CØNouıvıuu

LORRAIN ALLEN

Edited by: Maggie Kern
https://www.facebook.com/Ms.Kedits/

Proofread by: Shauna Stevenson
https://www.facebook.com/inkmachineediting/

Formatted by: Brenda Wright
https://www.facebook.com/FormattingDoneWright/

AUTHOR'S NOTE

This book features an out-of-control, jealous antihero, abuse, graphic language, explicit sex scenes, and other subject matters some readers might find triggering. Dominic Stone is not a comfortable antihero to read about. If you expect a redeemable antihero this book is not for you. He does NOT grovel or beg. Scan QR code to view content warning.

PLAYLIST

"Lick" – Joi
"Oops (Oh My)" – Tweet featuring Missy Elliott
"Motivation" – Kelly Rowland featuring Lil Wayne
"Drunk in Love" – Beyoncé featuring Jay Z
"Neighbors Know My Name" – Trey Songz
"Makin' Good Love" – Avant
"Signs of Love Makin'" – Tyrese
"Dirty" – Tank
"Fuckin' wit Me" – Tank
"Freek'N You" – Jodeci
"Anywhere" – 112
"Pony" – Ginuwine
"Wetter" – Twista
"My Body" – LSG
"Freak Me" – Silk
"Earned It" – The Weeknd
"Often" – The Weeknd
"The Birds (Part 2)" – The Weeknd

PROLOGUE

Dom

I glance at the fluffy white clouds visible from the window of my private jet. I've spent the past two weeks celebrating another year of life on my island in Belize with family and friends. The daily erotic escapades would make a porn star blush. Drinking, drugs, and orgies were in abundance. My narcotic of choice is warm, wet, and tight. I embrace being a perverted deviant. For the last few days, it's just been my companion and me. I needed to unwind before heading back to work.

At thirty-two years old, I'm the youngest self-made billionaire in the United States. Vacations, fast cars, endless women—I'm on top of the fucking world, living the high life in Los Angeles. What more could I ask for? I've been dubbed "The Forever Bachelor" by the media due to my very public playboy ways.

I come from humble beginnings, the second of three boys. My parents didn't have much. My father was a janitor and my mother was a housewife. Shit, they struggled to make ends meet, but our household never lacked love. They've been happily married for thirty-five years. I'm thrilled they've enjoyed marital bliss, but the thought of walking down the aisle doesn't appeal to me. I'll never be tied down by the ball and chain. I prefer variety, and there's no reason to limit my options.

I'm two hundred and twenty pounds of solid muscle, standing at six four. Throw in my amber eyes and dark blond hair, I'm a wet dream. But I'm more than just a handsome face and hot bod. At heart, I'm a computer geek who excelled in high school, which afforded me the opportunity to receive a partial scholarship to attend Princeton. My uncle, who passed a little over ten years ago, was the exact opposite of my father. Craig Stone was a go-getter who worked his way through college. Eventually, he became a major player on Wall Street, working as a financial advisor. Dad says I'm a replica of him, not just in looks, but in character and personality as well. My uncle and I were birds of a feather. Unfortunately, he and my father didn't get along. My good ole dad was too proud to accept monetary assistance from his younger brother, but if it weren't for him, I wouldn't be where I am today. At the time of his death, he didn't have a wife or kids, so his mini fortune was split between my brothers and me. Thus, Stone Incorporated was born; a successful multinational corporation based in Irvine, California. I'm in the business of creating servers, computers, and electronics. I'm a cocky, self-absorbed asshole, but hey, I have every right to be.

"We should go shopping when we get back home. Gucci's summer collection is to die for," Taylor says.

I turn my attention to my current fling. Taylor has the perfect ballerina body, golden hair bright as the sun, and crystal-clear blue eyes; she's absolutely gorgeous. The sex is phenomenal, but nonetheless, her time is up. It was good while it lasted. She's beginning to become clingy, and I can't have that. It'll lead to complications. She'll receive her walking papers once the jet lands at John Wayne Airport. I can't risk her having a tantrum while we're thousands of miles in the air.

"I'll see."

Her face frowns in dismay, but she quickly covers it up with a smile. "Okay, darling."

"Can I get you something else, sir?" Phoebe, the flight attendant, asks with a flirtatious glint in her eyes, causing Taylor to huff.

"Yes, I could use another scotch."

"My *pleasure*," she purrs.

Taylor dramatically clears her throat.

"Get me a bottled water," she snaps condescendingly.

Phoebe pastes on a fake smile. "Of course."

She walks away, adding an extra sway to her hips.

"How dare she openly flirt with you as if I wasn't sitting next to you?" Taylor shrills in outrage. "The little whore! I demand you fire her!"

I glower, baring my teeth. Her eyes widen in alarm. She's never seen this side of me. I'm usually a charming, carefree guy, unless someone crosses the line.

"You presume to dictate how I handle my employee?" I ask in a low but deadly tone.

"I'm sorry." She licks her lips anxiously. "I didn't mean to imply—"

Suddenly the jet rattles violently, sending Phoebe sprawling to the floor.

"What's happening?" Taylor screeches.

The aircraft stabilizes, and I instantly go to Phoebe's aid.

"I think my arm is broken," she screams, her face twisting in agony.

Fuck, it's twisted at an odd angle.

The pilot's voice blasts through the cabin. "Please fasten your seat belts. We may experience more turbulence."

"I'll make sure an ambulance is waiting for you when we land." I help her stand and guide her to a seat.

I buckle Phoebe in and hurry to my seat, strapping in right before the jet takes a nosedive.

"We're crashing!" Taylor yells at the top of her lungs.

I push her head down into her lap. "Don't move!" I shout.

I brace for impact, knowing this could very well be my final day on earth.

CHAPTER 1

Six years later

Pepper

The big day is here, and I couldn't be more excited. I was in total disbelief after receiving the acceptance email for the coveted *paid* software engineer intern position at Stone Incorporated. Today is new hire orientation. Working here and as a part-time waitress will keep me busy all summer.

The three-person panel interview took almost ninety minutes. They were very thorough in their questioning, wanting to ensure only the best moved forward. It was stressful, and I found myself stuttering through some of my responses, so I figured there was no way in heck I'd be considered. It wasn't that I didn't know my stuff, nervousness just got the better of me. I wanted to kick my own behind for screwing up so badly.

I'm in my sophomore year at Duncan University, studying computer science. Usually only graduating seniors are eligible to apply for the prestigious summer internship opportunities, but this year, the honor was extended to sophomores and juniors. The competition was fierce. I worked really hard for this by maintaining a high GPA throughout college thus far, in addition to volunteering at various community outreach centers around the city. Also, my professors provided glowing recommendation letters, which helped a lot.

I take one last look in the bathroom mirror, fluffing my kinky shoulder-length hair. Dark caramel-colored eyes set in a dark chocolate face stare back at me. My stomach is filled with butterflies.

Hearing the familiar tone of my cell phone, I walk into the bedroom and snag it from the dresser. I smile, seeing the name flashing across the small rectangular screen.

"Hi, Mia."

We met on the first day of freshmen year and became fast friends. She's actually my only friend. I was socially awkward. I'm grateful I had Mia to help me flourish. I didn't have the luxury of having a normal childhood, not with my strict upbringing by Pastor Russell Bryant. Even as an adult, he controls my life. He's an authoritarian. My theory is the military made him that way. As a former colonel in the United States Marine Corps, he demands unwavering obedience and rules with an iron fist.

College was my escape from his domineering guidance.

"Hey, just wanted to wish you luck."

"Thank you." I take a deep breath in the hopes of steadying my nerves. "I'm going to need it."

"You've got this," she assures me. "You're going to rock."

"I wish you were here."

"I know, babe, but we'll see each other when you come to visit in a few weeks."

Mia is originally from Denver and spends her summers there with her adoring family. I visited for a week last year to get away for a bit. It was refreshing to witness her family's playful banter, but it also made me sad. I lacked that type of affection since my mother died when I was eight years old. Mom was a free spirit. It's strange how two people who were so different ended up married. She chose the name Pepper because she said I added spice to her life. I miss her so much.

We were living in Buffalo, New York, when she was diagnosed with schizophrenia just after I turned five. The winters there are rough. One night, Mom left the house, disappearing into the blizzard with only her nightgown on. No one was the wiser until the morning. She was found frozen solid. Afterwards, my father uprooted my younger brother, Patrick, and me to the West Coast. He attends military school to jump-start his career in the service, leaving me alone and without a buffer against our father.

Another call beeps in, and I check the caller ID. "I'll call you during my lunch break. Dad's on the other line."

"Don't let the drill sergeant ruin your morning."

"I won't."

"Catch you later."

"Bye."

"Good morning," I greet my father in a chipper voice.

"Have you left for work yet?" he asks sternly, not bothering to return the salutation.

"I'm leaving as we speak." I grab my purse and keys and slide on my flats, then head out the door.

"That's not acceptable!" he shouts so loudly I tilt my head away from the phone. "It's six thirty, leaving you only an hour and a half to get to work."

"I'll be there in an hour with thirty minutes to spare." I made sure to time the commute perfectly.

"Always be prepared for the unexpected. A car accident or flat tire could cause you to be late. Remember—"

"If you're on time, you're late." Arriving fifteen minutes early is a requirement for him.

"Do not interrupt me when I'm speaking to you!" he barks.

"I'm sorry, Dad."

"Be sure it doesn't happen again. Patrick will get in this afternoon. I expect you here at seven for dinner."

"Yes, sir." I step into the elevator. "I have to—"

He hangs up before I can say goodbye.

I don't hate him, but I should. Without his guidance and financial support, I'm not sure where I'd be. He pays for college, bought me a car, and provides me a place to live. After retiring from the military, he purchased a few properties and became a landlord. I reside in a nice condo, rent- free, but I am responsible for paying utilities. Of course, he has a key and pops up unannounced, though he hasn't in a while.

He raised me with morals. Parties, revealing clothing, and boys were prohibited. In seventh grade, I had a crush on a classmate. I was ecstatic to learn he shared my affection. Unfortunately, we could only talk during school hours. One day, we were caught exchanging notes by the teacher. My plea for her not to call my father fell on deaf ears. I spent the remainder of the day in fear of what would happen once I got home. It was worse than I imagined.

Before stepping fully inside the house, I was slapped across the face with a hard object, sending me sprawling to the floor and causing my head to spin.

While cowering at my father's feet, I noticed he was holding a Bible. The Good Book had been used to deliver the blow.

"Harlot! You're a shameless whore, just like your mother!" he roared.

"I'm so sorry, Daddy."

"To keep you from temptation, you will be homeschooled, starting immediately."

"Please, no. It won't happen again."

"Now I will show you the repercussions of straying from the path of righteousness," he said, removing his belt.

I curled into a fetal position as he began to deliver stinging hits in quick succession all over my body. I screamed in agony, begging him to stop.

Eventually, he tired from the exertion and dragged my battered body inside the hall closet. He walked away, then reappeared with the Bible and a flashlight.

"You will stay locked in here for the entire weekend," he said, handing me both. "It must be done to save your soul from damnation. You will not be given food or water. Your only source of nourishment will be the word of God. Knock on the door if you need to use the bathroom."

"No, Daddy! Please!"

"Silence!" he bellowed, closing the door with a definitive click.

After that incident, I was required to recite Bible verses in the morning and before bedtime. Throughout the years, Dad regaled me with stories about my mother's supposed infidelities, saying she met her demise as punishment for her transgressions. My father prevented me from traversing the wrong path on numerous occasions. Because of him, I'm a good Christian woman and remain a virgin. Still, I'm constantly fighting to keep the unnatural hunger in me at bay. I crave his approval, but it seems I can't do anything right in his eyes. I'm going to try really hard to make him proud of me.

"Are you coming out?" a man asks.

"Sorry, I don't know where my mind is." I smile, stepping out of the elevator.

"Hey, it happens to us all, especially on Monday mornings." He walks into the elevator. "Have a good day."

"You too." I exit the building, then walk across the parking lot to my car.

CHAPTER 2

Dom

"Are you even listing to me?" Jensen asks.

I glance up from studying last quarter's earnings on the computer screen to glare at my big brother. "No."

He came barging into my office less than five minutes after I arrived and planted his ass in the plush leather chair in front of my desk.

"Sarah and I really want you to come over for dinner. It's been ages."

Jensen and Sarah met in college, and the rest is history. They're now at child number four. Three girls and a boy. They're probably done creating offspring since Jensen finally has the son he's coveted.

"You sure that's the best idea? Oliver screamed his head off the last time."

"Come on. That was nearly two years ago, and he was just a toddler. He would've gotten used to your appearance if you came around more."

My nephew had good reason to fear me. I sustained fourth-degree burns on the right side of my face from my temple to my neck. I'm so fucking grotesque, I can't stand to look at my own reflection. Mirrors are strictly prohibited in my residence.

I'll never forget the pain of my skin melting from the flames. Fortunately, I was able to undo my seat belt and drag myself from the wreckage. At that point, adrenaline kicked in and the pain was minimized. I must have passed out, because the next thing I remember is waking up in the hospital. I suffered a punctured liver, fractured leg, and several broken ribs. Sheet grafts were used to cover the burns, but the damage was too severe to help much. The pilot and Taylor died instantly. Phoebe was placed in a medically induced coma but later succumbed to her injuries.

Being the sole survivor plagues me with guilt to this day. What makes me so special? Why did I survive? It took months to recover, but I didn't return to the office for two years. The official investigation concluded the crash was caused due to pilot error.

"Don't you have to get to work?" I ask.

"My schedule is open until ten, and anyway, I always have time for my baby brother," Jensen replies.

"Well, mine isn't, so if you don't mind." I pointedly look from him to the door.

"How long do you plan on living this way?"

"What do you mean?" I ask, reclining in my executive chair.

"You've alienated yourself from your family."

"I'm busy running a billion-dollar company."

The immense office attests to my advanced wealth. Behind my Astoria Grand desk is a spectacular view of the skyline. Several-thousand-dollar paintings by artists who met their end long ago line the walls. A bar stocked with expensive liquor is to my left, and next to it is a door leading to a spacious studio apartment. During deadlines that require long nights, I sleep there instead of home. It has all the luxurious amenities someone of my station expects—a king-sized bed, a kitchenette featuring top-brand appliances, an Italian leather sofa situated in front of a coffee table and Persian rug, a flat-screen television mounted to the wall, a dinette set, two closets, and a bathroom.

"That's complete bullshit. Mom and Dad are worried about you. We all are."

"I can take care of myself."

"It's been six years."

"But it feels like it was yesterday," I snap. "What the fuck do you want from me, Jensen?"

"I want my brother back."

"The brother you knew died in the crash."

15

"No, he became bitter after he caught his fiancée fucking his best friend."

"I'm not in the mood to rehash the past," I growl, memories of that fateful day bombarding me.

Negotiations ended earlier than expected on a business trip in Beijing. I didn't tell Lauren, because I wanted to surprise her. Before boarding the plane to the States, I made a detour to a jewelry boutique, purchasing the most expensive tennis bracelet available as a gift for her. I showered her in luxury, grateful such a beautiful woman wanted to be with a monster. Anger barrels through me at the lovesick fool I was. Most women are gold-digging bitches aiming for a payday. No woman will ever be capable of looking past my burns. This is the face only a mother could love.

One year ago…

Foreboding filled me when I spotted Luke's car parked next to Lauren's in the circular driveway. Why is he here? Silently, I entered the mansion, not bothering to search the first floor. My gut told me exactly where they were. Slowly, I stalked up the stairs, careful to keep quiet. The unmistakable sound of sex intensified the closer I got to our bedroom. The door was slightly ajar, allowing me to watch my fiancée ride my best friend. She'd never ridden my dick so vigorously.

Murderous thoughts danced in my mind the longer I stood there. I wanted to grab a knife from the kitchen and carve their fucking hearts out. He flipped her over and thrusted his hips a few times before groaning. He rolled to his back, dragging in ragged breaths.

"Scarface will be home any day now," Luke joked.

"He makes me want to vomit." She shivered. "When he fucks me, I close my eyes and pretend it's you."

"Another year or so and it'll be over."

"That's easy for you to say," she snapped. "You don't have to fuck him."

"Look, everything's going according to plan. Marry the bastard next month, and a year later, file for a divorce."

"This scheme of yours better work."

"Dom's madly in love with you. He hasn't asked for a prenup, and he won't. You'll get half of his assets."

Instead of confronting them, I quietly left and began plotting my revenge. Luke arrived at work the following day only to be escorted from the building by security. The shocked expression on his face lessened the sting of his betrayal. I had the last laugh. Lauren was thrown out on her ass with nothing. Last

I heard, she's stripping at a club in downtown Los Angeles. I knew about her troubled past, but it didn't matter to me. I'd fallen for her hard. She was a damn good actress, playing me like a fucking fiddle. That incident desensitized me, turning me into an angry, black-hearted motherfucker with trust issues.

Luke and I became best friends in grade school and were inseparable. Though he wasn't qualified, I took a chance and gave him an executive position in my company. I had no idea he was envious of my wealth and wanted me to hit rock bottom.

"I'm sorry. I know that's a touchy subject for you." Jensen sighs.

"Yet you brought it up."

"You're not getting any younger."

"I knew this was coming. Did Mom put you up to this?"

"No. Well, maybe she voiced her concerns to me. You use women like they're disposable razors."

"What's wrong with that?"

Lauren was my first and only serious relationship. I'm a nightmare to every woman unlucky enough to cross my path. The hole between their legs is my only interest. No wining and dining, flowers, or fucking chocolates. My cock is all I offer. There's one cardinal rule I follow to a T—never fuck the same woman twice. No attachments or expectations—well, on my part. One-night stands work perfectly fine for me. Eventually, I'll get married for the sole purpose of continuing my legacy. The marriage will be a business arrangement, nothing more.

"Sarah has a coworker who is perfect for you."

"Bad idea."

"What?" Jensen asks.

"Trying to hook me up with Sarah's coworker."

"Why?"

"Do you really need to ask?" I deadpan.

"One blind date isn't going to kill you."

"True, but it'll kill you for sure."

"What do you mean?" He scrunches his eyebrows.

"Sarah will murder you once I fuck her coworker, then ignore her calls."

"Really, Dom?" He scowls. "You'd do that?"

A knock sounds at the door.

"Come in," I call.

Peggy, my administrative assistant, sticks her head inside. "I'm sorry for the interruption. Mr. Jamison is here for the nine o'clock meeting. He's waiting in conference room A."

"I'll be right there," I tell her, then turn back to my brother. "We'll have to finish this discussion another day."

"I agree, but tonight over dinner works for me."

"I'll think about it." I stand, happy to end the conversation.

"No, you won't."

"Keep hope alive." I wink at him, then gladly leave my office.

Pepper

I arrive at Stone Incorporated ahead of schedule. I've seen pictures of the immaculate Plexiglas structure online and in business magazines, but seeing it up close and personal takes my breath away. Stone Inc. graces the front in gleaming silver letters. The rectangular fourteen-story building covers an entire block. I enter the lobby where close to one hundred interns are gathered. I definitely stick out like a sore thumb. Everyone is so sophisticated in their chic corporate attire, and I'm drab in my loose-fitting plain black dress and "grandma" church shoes.

Maybe it's time my wardrobe received an upgrade.

The thought of my father's reaction vanquishes the idea instantly. He'd call me a vain sinner. Maybe I'll casually mention it at dinner later.

"Good morning, everyone," an older woman sporting a sleek bun and wearing a black pantsuit

21

announces. "My name is Vivian Buchanan. I work in employee relations, and I'll be your tour guide this morning. Please follow me."

The modern office features luxurious furniture, height-adjustable desks, and ergonomic chairs for a comfortable working environment. The icing on the cake for me is the swimming pool, gym, and huge cafeteria with several food stations to choose from. Those are only a few perks the company has to offer. We are now being taken to a room with an auditorium-style setup. On top of each desk is a Beacon Pro X, the latest laptop assembled by Stone's computer-build technicians.

One look at the agenda and my excitement increases tenfold. The genius himself will be addressing the group at eleven thirty. I spend the next two hours completing new hire paperwork and learning company policies. Finally, we're granted a ten-minute break, and I go to the employee lounge. I immediately eye the tasty donuts on the counter. Not too long ago, I shamelessly scarfed down two. Eating another one would totally be pushing my daily calorie intake. These hips are wide enough.

"Pepper."

"Yes?" I turn from the fried deliciousness to a vaguely familiar face. He's tall, tan, with jet-black hair and gray eyes. We look to be similar in age.

"I thought I recognized you."

"Have we met?" I can't place him.

"We went to Duncan University together until I graduated last year."

A light clicks on in my head. "Camden?"

"Yeah." He openly ogles my chest. "So, you're interning here for the summer?"

He invited me to a few parties at his frat house, but I always declined. I promised my father to focus on my studies and not to engage in the typical college life. My answer wouldn't have changed regardless. Camden gave me the creeps with the way his eyes undressed me, much like he's doing at this exact moment. I never understood his interest in me. One day, he sat next to me in the library and started a conversation. We bumped into each other from time to time on campus after that.

"Yep. I'm really stoked."

"If you want someone to show you the ropes, I'm your man."

"Thanks. I'll keep that in mind."

"Do you want to grab a bite to eat later and catch up?"

"I can't. I'm having dinner with the family."

"Are you free tomorrow night?"

"I'll have to check my schedule."

I'm such a wuss. Being straight up and telling him I'm not interested would put an end to him asking again. My problem is, I hate hurting people's feelings, but more times than not, I find myself in the hot seat because of it.

"Okay," he says, disappointment clear in his voice.

"Well, I better head back."

"See you around."

"Yeah."

Dom

At the announcement of my arrival, I receive a standing ovation. My eyes roam over the enthusiastic faces of the young and impressionable as I walk to the front of the room.

"Good morning," Keisha, an employee from the human resources department, greets.

I nod, standing behind the podium. The audience watches me expectantly, waiting for words of wisdom. I remember being like them—ready to take on the universe—but lately, I've been restless. The monotony of my daily activities is starting to grate on my nerves. I'm missing passion and excitement in my life. I need a challenge. I'm supposed to pump up the new recruits, get them thrilled about the prospect of a career at Stone Inc. by explaining how hard work and dedication pays off. I'm usually all for the dog and pony show, since talent is important for growth and blowing the competition out of the water, but it wouldn't be good for my turbulent attitude to be sensed by the interns. The speech will be short and to the point.

Consumed

"Welcome to Stone Incorporated. Each of you is sitting here today because you made a lasting impression on the recruitment team. They saw greatness in you. Building this company from the ground up was no easy feat. I encountered numerous obstacles and repeated failures, but I remained resilient…"

Twenty minutes later, my speech is concluded, and I receive another standing ovation as I exit the room.

I'm horny as shit. That's probably why I'm antsy. I'll stop by Secrets, a high-class gentleman's club for the uber rich, and be balls deep in some pussy by midnight. Fucking until the wee hours of the morning should ease my frustrations. I'm well-known, but even if I weren't, it's easy for women to spot power and wealth. They're all too willing to overlook my scars in the hopes of obtaining a piece of it.

CHAPTER 4

Pepper

On the drive to Dad's, my thoughts wander to Dominic Stone. His piercing eyes, chiseled jaw, Greek nose, and full lips add to his male beauty, despite the marred skin covering the right side of his face. He has an intimidating countenance. Though his words were encouraging, the subtle hints of his body language told the story of a restless soul. Being one myself, it wasn't hard to recognize him as a kindred spirit.

I pull into the driveway of my childhood residence and turn the engine off. It always takes me a few minutes to compose myself before going inside. A person's home should be their sanctuary from the unpleasantness of the world. For me, it was a prison. Attending school was a refuge for me until my father forbade it, convinced I would be corrupted. Being retired, he devoted his time to homeschooling me. Bible study was a major part of the daily curriculum.

Every scripture is ingrained in my brain. I missed out on so much—prom, graduation, a first kiss.

Memories assail me, causing me to hyperventilate. I breathe in deeply in an effort to calm my racing heart and still my shaky body.

I only visit when summoned, staying only long enough to appease my father. I'm happy my brother, Patrick, is home for the summer. His presence will make being here easier. Most likely, I won't see him too often once he graduates high school next year.

I scream when a sharp knock startles me, dissipating my thoughts. Lester, a deacon at Dad's church, profusely apologizes through the window. He's a tall, thin man. I probably outweigh him by twenty pounds. Though only in his mid-thirties, he's already experiencing male-pattern baldness. His lips are always dry, and white foam forms at the corners of his mouth. Seeing it makes me queasy. In church, he's always touchy-feely, and the way his beady eyes roam my body makes me uncomfortable.

I step out of my car. "You almost gave me a heart attack."

"I noticed you sitting there and wanted to check if you were okay."

"I'm fine. Just talking to old ghosts."

"I hope they're the good ones."

"Do good ghosts exist?"

"I think so."

"What are you doing here?"

Don't look at the white foam, don't look at the white foam, don't look at the white foam… Dang it, I looked at the white foam.

"Your father invited me to dinner."

"Oh. He didn't mention we were having a guest."

"Maybe it slipped his mind."

I find that hard to believe. He forgets nothing.

"Shall we go in?" I ask, walking to the front door.

"Sure. Congratulations on finishing the semester with stellar grades and starting a new internship today."

"Thanks."

My father emerges from the kitchen when we enter the house. His once muscular physique is gone. His midsection rivals Santa Claus, but it doesn't make him any less fearsome.

He gives me a peck on the cheek and Lester a firm handshake. "I hope you're hungry. I cooked a good, hearty meal."

"It smells delicious. What are we having?" Lester asks.

"Roast beef, carrots, and potatoes."

"Hey, sis!" Patrick flies down the stairs, envelopes me in a bear hug, and swings me around.

Man, he must be a foot taller than the last time I saw him. I'm amazed at how grown-up and handsome he is. We have the same dark complexion, but that's where our similarities end. His eyes are deep brown, and he has the cutest dimples. He'll definitely need a broom to beat the girls off.

I return the embrace, squealing in delight. "Jeez, you're a giant. What are you now? Six two?"

"Put her down!" Dad snaps, and just like that, he ruins our reunion.

"I'm just excited. I haven't seen Pepper since New Year's Day," he protests.

"That's no excuse to behave like a wild animal."

"Whatever," Patrick mumbles.

He puts me on my feet and heads to the dining room. We follow behind and sit at the table. Dad says grace, then we dig in.

"Lester received a promotion to branch manager at the bank where he works," Dad says.

"Congrats. We both have accomplishments to celebrate."

"What are you celebrating?" Patrick asks.

"I started an internship at Stone Incorporated today."

"Wow! The owner is a gazillionaire. I would love to get my hands on the new Beacon," Patrick says, rubbing his palms together.

"He's an exceptional, God-fearing man and has a great head on his shoulders," Dad says, reverting the discussion back to Lester.

"Maybe you can approve me for a personal loan." Patrick grins, wiggling his eyebrows at Lester.

I laugh internally. He's incorrigible. I love when he's home.

Dad bangs his fist on the table. "Control your mouth or you can dismiss yourself."

"It's a joke. Chill." Patrick throws his fork on his plate and stands. "I need to finish unpacking."

During Patrick's visits, he and Dad bicker nonstop. It's the reason he chose not to come home for spring vacation and stayed at a friend's instead.

Why can't I be brave like Patrick? I've never had the stomach to talk back to our father, maybe because I faced his harshness every day and had no one to rely on for support. I learned to listen because the alternative was corporal punishment.

I grab his wrist when he stomps past me. "I'll come up before I leave."

He nods.

Fantastic. Now I'm left with these two. I need to make my exit sooner rather than later.

"Any woman would be blessed to have Lester as a husband," my father remarks.

I choke on my lemonade. Whoa, that comment came out of nowhere.

"Oh. Have you found a lucky lady to propose to?" I ask.

Is my father playing matchmaker? The conversation is treading into dangerous territory if he is.

"Not yet, but your father has told me about your exemplary morals." Lester smiles, showing crooked yellow teeth. "I was hoping we could become better acquainted outside of church. Maybe you'll be the *lucky lady* one day."

White foam.

"Oh… well… um… Dad wants me to focus on school."

I see this man on Wednesdays for Bible study and on Sundays. That's the extent of our association. There's no attraction... no spark, and he's super creepy.

"Nonsense. Lester is a prime catch. You can't let him slip through your fingers."

All of a sudden, he's fine with me dating, as long as he selects the man.

"Are you free Friday night?" Lester asks.

"I… um… have…"

"She's available." Dad narrows his eyes at me.

"Wonderful! I'll pick you up at six."

"Mmm… okay."

"It's settled then," Dad states, considering the matter closed, and resumes eating his meal. I'm such a coward. It's clear he wants me to date and eventually marry Lester.

What am I going to do?

On the drive home, I berate myself for agreeing to a date with Lester. Then I think, *What if he's the man God sent for me?* Maybe it wouldn't hurt to give him a chance, but the white foam flashes in my mind's eye.

Yuck.

After getting home, I take a long, hot shower before settling in bed. I lie propped against the pillows, writing in my diary. It's the keeper of my deep dark secrets and ongoing fantasies. The contents should've caused the pages to go up in flames long ago. My education of sex was acquired through television, porn, and Mia. Only she is privy to my ungodly desires. I'm afraid to confide in anyone else, afraid of being judged. She encourages me to experiment, but that means I'll have to commit a sin. I'm supposed to remain virtuous until I'm married. Every day, I pray for God to deliver my soul from the clutches of Satan.

At night when I close my eyes, seeking slumber, I dream of a faceless man who plays a recurring role in my subconscious mind. He lures me to the abyss, promising ecstasy beyond my wildest imagination. I glance left to the beckoning light beseeching me to enter eternal grace. Then I peer right, towards darkness. There, the stranger looms, holding his hand out for me. Though he doesn't physically touch me, somehow his caress is tangible. It floats across my flushed flesh and sends a zing of electricity straight to my center. Unconsciously, I wander to him. I can't resist; my body is weak.

He makes love to me. Every kiss, every touch, every thrust, transports me closer to the point of no return. I gladly give him ownership of my soul, choosing Hell over Heaven. God tests me, and I fail each time. Then I wake, sweaty and throbbing between my legs. I pray immediately, asking for forgiveness. How can I crave something I've never had? Want a man I've never seen? I've always fought this battle within me. My father said I have my mother's sickness.

One day my curiosity got the better of me. My father left home to run an errand, leaving me to my own devices. The memory still haunts me.

I watched from my bedroom window as Dad's car disappeared down the street. Once the coast was clear, I gathered my courage, laid on the bed, and slid my hand under the waistband of my panties. I explored tentatively at first, then became bolder, spreading my legs farther apart as the pleasure increased. My hips began to rock in sync with my plundering fingers, becoming lost in blissful self-discovery. I was very close to reaching something magical when my father entered the room.

"Unholy, impure harlot!" he shouted, dragging me off the bed.

"I'm sorry!" I said, more frightened than I've ever been in my life.

He pulled me down the stairs and into the kitchen where he turned on the burner and held the underside of my wrist over the flame.

"Daddy! No!" I screamed, trying to break his hold.

"Satan has taken hold of you!"

"I'll never touch there again! Daddy, please!"

"That is what Hell feels like!" He threw me to the floor. "You have your mother's sickness in you."

I withered in pain, squeezing myself into a tiny ball, petrified of what would come next. I heard something being dumped onto the ceramic tile before I was yanked to my knees. Rice littered the floor.

"Kneel on the rice," he demanded. "You will stay this way all night and pray for your wicked soul."

Dad had forgotten his wallet in his room and had come back home. I was so focused on the pleasure; I didn't hear his return.

I absentmindedly skim my thumb over the slightly raised skin under my wrist. The scarring is barely noticeable. My father had treated the injury himself, saying I only received second-degree burns, so there was no need to seek medical attention. But I knew his decision not to go had more to do with not being able to explain how I obtained the burn. I began touching myself again about a year ago. There was no risk of being caught unawares late at night in the privacy of my condo. It's become an addiction I can't conquer.

Consumed

The sounds of sex penetrate the thin walls of my bedroom. My neighbor's girlfriend must be staying the night. I look forward to Kaci's visits. The couple has a voracious sexual appetite and spend hours making love. Most people would be livid for being kept from sleep, but not me. Listening to them makes me feel alive. I imagine it's me he's pleasuring, my name he shouts as he reaches climax. I've seen him around the building, even rode the elevator with him a few times. He's an attractive man—tall, bald with a goatee, and toffee-colored skin. I've never seen Kaci, but I envision she's beautiful. My breaths come in short, shallow pants as a tingling sensation spreads through my private area. I get out of bed and hurry to the other side of my bedroom. I eagerly press my ear to the cool wall. Their grunts and moans invade my senses. I close my eyes and delve my hand into my bottoms. My fingers rapidly knead my clit.

"Julian! Fuck me harder, faster!" Kaci screams.

The squeaking noise of the bed intensifies as he grants her request.

"I'm about to come, babe!" he roars.

They shout, reaching their end together.

I slide to the floor, trembling from the onslaught of my own orgasm.

I'm a dirty whore, just like my father has accused me of being numerous times.

I head to the bathroom on wobbly legs to wash away my shame.

Dom

Not one of the superficial bitches at the gentleman's club appealed to me, so I went without. Since then, I've been more irritable and snapping at everyone. Fuck, I need some pussy. It's ten o'clock, and I'm just getting to work. I even missed an important meeting. Employees avoid me as I stride towards my office, sensing my turbulent mood. I don't blame them.

"Pepper's a virgin." I hear a man say just before I pass the employee lounge.

Curiosity piqued; I stop to eavesdrop on the conversation.

"Yeah, right, man," another man scoffs. "Most girls lose their virginity by age fifteen nowadays."

"Not this one. She was homeschooled and kept sheltered. Her old man is a pastor and a real hard case."

"How do you know all of this?"

"A friend's girlfriend and Pepper were partners on a class project. They got a little close, and one day she spilled the beans."

"I'm pretty sure she's fucked someone by now."

"I doubt it, but I'll find out soon enough."

"That's if she wants you," the guy says.

"Her interning here is the perfect opportunity for me. I'll have her by the end of the summer, guaranteed," he gloats.

So, a churchgoing virgin is within my reach.

Is she corruptible? That's the question of the hour. It seems my hunt for a challenge has landed on my doorstep. Lucky me. I just need to figure out who she is and if the sheltered princess interests me.

"Care to place a wager?" the first man asks.

"You're on."

It's time for me to put a halt to this discussion.

"Gentlemen," I say, entering the room to find both men dawdling by the coffee machine.

They look vaguely familiar, but there are over fifteen thousand employees at this location alone, so it's impossible to recall the names of everyone I don't work with directly.

"Good morning." From the sound of his voice, this is the one who plans to make Pepper his conquest.

"What's your name?"

"Camden Bailey," he answers nervously.

"And yours?"

"Levi Colton."

"Is it lunchtime already?" I ask sharply.

"N-no," Camden stutters.

"Then get back to work. You're not paid to gossip."

They scramble from the room like headless chickens.

It's coincidence I happened upon this exchange. My office is on the top floor, but I stopped at this level to speak with the infrastructure supervisor.

It's time for the little virgin and I to become acquainted. I whistle, sauntering down the hall, my disposition improving drastically.

Everyone turns their attention to me when I enter the conference room. "I didn't mean to interrupt."

"Your presence is always welcome," Lloyd, the software engineer manager, assures.

My sole purpose for making an appearance is to catch a glimpse of the woman who's been at the forefront of my mind since this morning.

"Continue. I'm just here to observe," I tell him.

He nods and resumes the presentation.

There's no empty space at the oval table but no matter. I'd rather study her from afar without being inhibited. I move to the back and lean against the wall. As I study the faces in the room, my gaze clashes with hers.

She smiles shyly, bewitching me before quickly turning away. She'd reserve it for someone more deserving if she knew what I had in store for her.

While reading through her electronic file, I came across her driver's license. The image wasn't large enough for me to really examine her features, but now I have free rein to do so. She's radiant. Silky dark skin, slightly arched eyebrows, captivating golden-brown orbs framed by thick eyelashes, a small, pert nose, and full, heart-shaped lips that belong around my cock. She's only twenty, making me eighteen years her senior.

Pepper exudes innocence, triggering my beast to perk up and mark her as prey. An uncontrollable need to corrupt her assails me. Most people fight their primitive urges, afraid of being judged, but I welcome mine with open arms and even offer it a damn drink. I've been accused of being a nymphomaniac and a sadist by past lovers. I don't deny their claims. Fucking and inflicting pain is my obsession. I dabble in the taboo often, continuously testing the limits of my depravity.

Pepper's virginity is my property, and I'll claim it at length. I've gleaned basic information from her file, so I'll have to take a more direct approach to get to know the real Pepper Bryant. I'll lure the pastor's daughter to the dark side in due time.

"All right, it's quitting time. Have a great weekend," Lloyd says. "Remember to submit ideas by close of business on Wednesday."

The group disbands. Some of the bolder team members try to engage in idle chitchat with me, but I'm focused on her. Noting my demeanor, the attempts are short-lived.

She looks to be close to five six, a bit above average in height compared to her counterparts. A gold necklace adorns her slender neck, with a cross pendant resting at the base of her throat. I leisurely peruse her curvaceous physique from top to bottom.

Pepper's lavender-colored dress accentuates her hourglass figure and almost has me unloading in my slacks. She's heavier than the women I usually fuck. I put her near one fifty, give or take a few pounds, but she carries her weight well. I could lose myself in those big juicy tits, plump ass, and thick thighs. She's ripe as fuck, ready for her cherry to be popped and eaten. I covertly watch her until she leaves the room.

"Great meeting," I say, ambling up to Lloyd.

Stroking his ego is a good way to steer the conversation in the direction I want it to go.

"Thank you." He puffs out his chest at the compliment.

"Are the interns assigned to you performing satisfactorily?"

"Absolutely."

"I hear Pepper Bryant is a go-getter," I state nonchalantly, not wanting to alert him to my interest in her.

"She's timid, but as the week's progressed, I've discovered she's a bright, vivacious young woman."

"Excellent. The choice to extend internships to sophomores and juniors wasn't taken lightly."

"It was an awesome decision. I better get going. I promised the family I'd take them roller-skating this evening."

"Have fun."

"I won't, but the kids will." He laughs. "See you Monday."

Once he's out of sight, I walk over to the chair Pepper occupied. I never thought I'd be jealous of an inanimate object. I kneel and place my hand on the seat, finding it still warm from her body heat. My cock grows to full length.

Heel, boy. You'll get a taste soon enough.

I bury my nose into the cushion and inhale her lingering vanilla scent.

Mission Deflower Pepper starts tonight.

CHAPTER 6

Pepper

The day I've been dreading is here; my date with Lester. He sat beside me during Bible study Wednesday night and acted as if we were already a couple. Some church members even commented how cute we were. My father is thrilled. He called and demanded I wear something nice. I chose a simple white sundress and yellow sandals.

He should be here in ten minutes. This is going to be a disaster. I need to put my foot down with Dad. I don't see Lester as my future mate. There is absolutely nothing drawing me to him. We have nothing in common, so I'm at a complete loss as to what we'll talk about. I'm horrible at forced conversations.

I lie down on the sofa, waiting on him to call. Though I insisted on driving myself, he wouldn't hear of it, making an awkward situation worse.

My phone rings. It's probably him. I pull it from my purse and see its Mia.

"Hello?" I answer, relieved. Talking to her always puts me in a better mood.

"Hey. Just wanted to check in and see how your first week went."

"Amazing. My input is valued, which is really great, and my supervisor is amazing."

"Awe-some," she sings. "Meet any cute guys?"

I instantly think of Mr. Stone. My face heated when he caught me staring at him, so I smiled and quickly looked forward. It could be my overactive imagination, but I felt his eyes on me, similar to the way the unknown man in my dreams caresses my body without actually touching me. I didn't look back to confirm, too chicken to get caught ogling him again.

"N-not really," I stutter.

"Are you lying to me, Pepper Bryant?" Mia asks cheekily.

Telling white lies to her is impossible.

"I think Dominic Stone is kind of handsome." I downplay that he's super attractive to me.

"He's like fifty!" she screeches. "Old enough to be your father, and he has those hideous scars."

"He's not that old."

"So, are you planning on losing your virginity to a grandpa?"

"No. I find him attractive, that's all. Anyway, he wouldn't be interested in me, and I'm only having sex after marriage."

"Oh my God."

"Don't use the Lord's name in vain."

"Enough. You're getting laid when you get here. I have a new neighbor who looks like Henry Cavill and he's single. You won't hesitate to drop those drawers when you meet him, honey."

"You're wiggling your eyebrows, aren't you?" I deadpan.

She snorts in laughter. "Yep. You know me too well."

"I'm not having a one-night stand."

"You're going to be here for a week, so it doesn't have to be just one night. It can be several."

There's a knock at the door.

"I have to go. Lester's here," I say on a sigh.

"Wait. What? I thought you were going to tell your dad to shove it."

"I was—"

"But you chickened out," Mia says in disappointment.

"Unfortunately."

"Do what makes *you* happy. You only have one life. If you want to fuck, fuck. You want to get drunk, bottoms up. Hell, if you want to run down Hollywood Boulevard in your birthday suit, do it."

I laugh. "I'm pretty sure that last one would land me in jail."

"And? Live a little. It'll be a hell of a story to tell your grandkids."

"I promise I'll stand up to him soon."

She lets out a breath. "Enjoy your date from hell."

"Yeah, yeah."

I end the call and go open the door.

"You look absolutely stunning," Lester says, handing me a bouquet of red roses.

"Thank you. Let me put these in water, then we can head out."

"All right."

The drive was as uncomfortable as I'd envisioned. It's a relief we're going to a play after dinner since we can't talk during the performance, but there is the intermission. I could excuse myself and hide out in the bathroom until it's over.

We're at an Italian restaurant. Dad must've told him it's my favorite food to eat. The carbonara smells wonderful, but my appetite is nonexistent. I pick through the pasta, wishing for the conclusion of this night to speed up.

"You look really beautiful tonight," he says for the tenth time since I got into his car.

"Umm... thanks."

We lapse into silence again. I can't take this anymore.

"You can order something else if you'd like." He nods towards my plate.

"It's good. I ate too much at lunch."

"You can get a to-go box."

"I'll do that." I take a sip of my Sprite.

"I'm looking forward to spending a lot more time with you."

My drink goes down the wrong pipe, causing me to cough uncontrollably.

"Are you okay?" he asks, concern etched on his face.

"Yeah," I croak.

"Initially I had reservations about asking you out, figuring I wouldn't be your type, but your father assured me I'm the kind of man you need."

"Shouldn't we head to the theater?"

I'd rather endure the awkward silence than this line of conversation.

"Oh, you're right. I completely lost track of time." He signals the waiter.

Continuing with this farce is going to require superb acting skills.

Dom

I've been following Pepper all week to gauge her habits and patterns. It's obvious she wants to be anywhere but here. Her date is too dumb to notice. I recognize him from the church on Wednesday night. He walked Pepper to her car.

Maybe she's using him for her own selfish gain. It wouldn't surprise me; women are deceptive. Why else would Pepper agree to a date with a man she isn't interested in?

I tailed the pair from her condo to the restaurant. I took a risk coming inside, but it's not uncommon for people who work together to bump into each other outside the office. I requested a table where my observations wouldn't be obstructed but far away enough to evade detection. If she spotted me, I'd play it off as a coincidence. Once they left, I acted quickly to avoid losing them.

Unable to trail them inside their next destination, I opt to go back to her condo for a sneak peek at her personal abode. I stop by the hardware store to purchase a set of hex wrenches. Using it and a credit card grants me access to Pepper's dwelling.

The lights are on, which is a plus for me. I walk through the compact space. The living and dining room are combined. Furniture is sparse—an ugly as hell purple sofa, coffee table, an outdated television, and a rickety white table. Family and Christian-themed photos dot the walls.

Fascinating. Maybe Pepper is a good girl after all, or a bad girl pretending to be good. Either way, I'm making it a priority to find out. I spot the kitchen to the left as I walk down the short hall, but that doesn't interest me, so I keep moving. To the right is the bathroom. The clothes she wore today lie discarded on the floor. I pick up her pink panties. The word *Friday* is on the front—cute. I bring the cotton to my nose, sniffing the decadent scent. Groaning, I savor the mouthwatering aroma. My cock expands to full mast, straining against my zipper for freedom. I lick the crotch of her panties, swallowing her fragrant flavor. Stuffing the thin material into my pocket, I proceed to her bedroom. Her vanilla smell permeates the air.

"Holy fuck," I say, peering at the large cross hanging above her bed.

There's not much furniture in here either, only three pieces—a maple-colored dresser, nightstand, and bed. I rummage through her drawers but find nothing intriguing. I'm done here for now. As I leave her bedroom, the hamper catches my eye. I dump the contents on the floor, then gather all of Pepper's dirty panties and stuff them into my pockets. After putting her clothes back to rights, I leave the condo.

Pepper

"By the way, I found a job for the summer," Patrick says around a mouthful of eggs.

We sit at the table, enjoying the big breakfast I cooked for us this morning.

"Congrats. Didn't realize you were looking for one."

"I wasn't but saw the help wanted sign posted in the window and thought, 'Why the hell not?'"

"Where?"

"The smoothie shop a couple blocks from here."

"My all-time favorite place?" I ask excitedly.

"Yeppers. I start next week, and you can use my employee discount."

"How much?"

"Twenty percent."

"Yay!" I jump up and do an uncoordinated dance.

He laughs at my antics.

"So, how did your date with your dream guy go last night?" he asks, killing the mood.

"Do not go there." I plonk back down in my chair and throw a sausage at him. "I invited you over so we could catch up, not talk about Lester."

"You should've told Dad to kiss your ass."

"Hey, watch your language."

"Yes, ma'am. I'll keep it PG." He gulps down the rest of his orange juice. "You and Lester don't mesh at all."

"I'll talk to Dad, just not now. It's too soon."

"Why do you let him control your life?"

"Don't judge me. You were safely at military school while I was stuck with him."

"Tell me what happened," he says, reaching across the table and squeezing my hand. "What did he do to you?"

Though Patrick comes home for holidays and summer vacation, he never witnessed our father's harsher punishments. Dad's careful to hide his abusive nature.

"I will one day."

"All right. I'm all ears when you're ready."

"Thanks."

"I have some news to tell you," he says, a wide smile on his face.

"What?"

"I'm not joining the military."

"I don't understand. It's been your dream forever."

"That's the thing. A military career isn't for me. It's what Dad wants. He's driven me towards it my whole life, and I'm tired of him pushing his bullshit agenda on me."

"When will you tell him?"

"After graduation."

"What are your plans?"

"I have no clue. The sky is the limit. I'm definitely not enrolling in college for a year or two. I need to figure out what motivates me."

"That's awesome." I pause. "He'll be livid."

"I don't give a crap."

"You have my full support."

"That means a lot, sis."

"You can always count on me. Now, finish your breakfast. My goal to slim down these hips begins today."

"You joined a gym?"

"Nope. I'm going jogging," I say proudly.

"You? Jogging? Good luck."

"Have some faith in your sister." I scowl playfully, this time throwing a potato at him.

It feels good to have my brother back.

I'm not accustomed to dining at chain restaurants, but I'm not here to enjoy the food. Pepper is working tonight, giving me the chance to interact with her.

Pepper stops, pausing for a few seconds when she sees me sitting at a table in her section before continuing forward. The white polo shirt and black pants she's wearing mold to her lush curves.

"Hi," she says nervously. "You probably don't recognize me—"

"You're an intern at my company."

"Yes." She glances away shyly. "My name is—"

"Pepper Bryant."

She nods. "I'm surprised you know who I am."

"Your supervisor sings your praises."

She clasps her hands together and bites her full bottom lip in exhilaration. "Mr. Stone, I'm delighted to intern for such an amazing corporation."

"You deserve it, and please, call me Dom."

She smiles. "Okay."

Her innocence is fucking seductive. Pepper is capable of seducing a man with little to no effort at all. That makes her dangerous.

"It doesn't disturb you to look at my face?"

"No. Should it?"

"It's not easy for most people to stare at an ugly mug like mine."

"I think you're handsome." Her eyes widen in embarrassment. "I'm sorry, I shouldn't have said that."

"I abhor liars," I growl. "No sane person would consider me handsome."

"I'm not lying." Her voice trembles.

I study Pepper intently, aiming to decipher the truth of her words.

"Have you decided?" She gestures towards the menu, breaking the tension.

"Not yet. What do you recommend?"

"The barbeque bacon cheeseburger is one of my favorites."

"Then I'll have that."

"How would you like your burger?"

"Rare."

"Regular or sweet potato fries for an extra two dollars and seventy-nine cents?"

"Regular is fine."

"Drink?"

"Heineken."

"I'll be right back."

Damn, that's a whole lot of ass; it bounces with each step she takes. I can't wait to bend her over and fuck her virgin cunt.

She returns, placing the beer on the table. I notice her hand is shaky. "Here you go."

I grab her wrist. "Do I frighten you?"

"Of course not."

I tighten my grip. "I won't tolerate being lied to. This is your last warning."

"You're a bit intimidating," she replies, eyes downcast.

"Regrettably, I can't alleviate your fears." My thumb glides across the rapidly beating pulse in her wrist before I place a kiss there. "Excelling at intimidation is one of the many reasons I'm successful. Also, it pleasures me to see people squirm."

She snatches her arm from my hold.

"I should see if your food is ready," she says, fleeing.

Another waitress brings my food to the table.

"Where's Pepper?"

"On a break. Is there anything I can get you?"

"Yeah. Pepper."

"Umm… okay."

She's still absent almost a half hour later. If Pepper thinks I won't seek her out, she underestimated me. I head to the kitchen, spotting her immediately when I push through the double doors.

"You can't be back here," she whispers.

It's too busy for anyone to notice a stranger in their midst. At my approach, she backpedals, but I seize her hips, pulling her close until there's no space between us. She lets out a small whimper.

"You need to work on your customer service skills," I growl.

"C-cadence is t-taking c-care of you," she stammers.

"You're my waitress, not her. Do your damn job and *serve* me. Or should I cause a scene?"

"No."

"Good. Tell your coworker she's no longer required. Got it?"

"Yes."

Satisfied with her response, I exit the kitchen. Pepper appears within minutes but keeps her distance.

"Why were you avoiding me?" I ask.

"I felt uncomfortable."

"Explain."

"You kissed my wrist."

"Is that a crime?"

"It's not appropriate."

"Follow me to the restroom, and I'll show you inappropriate."

She inhales sharply. "Mr. Stone—"

"Dom."

"Is there anything else I can get for you?" she asks, flashing me an incensed glare.

Your pussy on a platter.

"No," I reply, giving her a credit card.

Pepper almost bumps into a customer in her effort to get away. She's back in record time, slamming the receipt and pen down before hurrying to take the order of a couple and doesn't spare me another glance. Her indignant outrage amuses me.

The chase has begun. My prey is on the run, but she'll be captured eventually. I pull an envelope from my billfold and lay it on the table. The first move has been made.

CHAPTER 8

Pepper

I've been distracted all day. My father called to reprimand me for not actively participating in church or staying after to talk with Lester, but images of *him* permeated my thoughts.

Dom is commanding, enigmatic, and scary. I swear there was fire dancing in his bright amber eyes. He makes me think bad things—sinful things. His disfigurement doesn't take away from his masculine beauty.

Last night, I dreamed of him. The man who takes over my subconscious mind now has a face. I want to experience his full lips on mine. My center throbs recalling his mouthwatering rosewood scent. He's a temptation sent to test my faith.

I glance at the envelope holding ten thousand dollars lying on the coffee table. Once Dom left, I went to collect the receipt and found the envelope bearing my name next to it. I've been lounging on the sofa, obsessing over this since arriving home instead of starting my chores. Tomorrow morning, I'll go straight to his office and confront him.

Decision settled, I click off the television and head to my room to fold laundry. I'm just about finished with the task when I notice my panties are missing; all except for the pair I wore Friday night. I washed the clothes yesterday after work, but the encounter with Dom shook me, so I wasn't completely lucid. It's possible I forgot them somehow. I take the stairs to the first floor where the laundry room is located and search the machine but find nothing. *Strange.* Back inside my condo, I hunt for the undergarments with no luck.

Did someone steal them from the washer or dryer? That's creepy. I guess this mystery will never be solved. I flop down on my bed and call Mia. She didn't make a peep as I recounted my run-in with Dom.

"Are you fucking for real!" she shouts.

"Language."

"Oh, hush, girl. This qualifies as a 'fuck' moment."

I roll my eyes, though she can't see the gesture. "What should I do?"

"Keep the money, duh!" she squawks. "You're out of your mind if you give it back."

"It's wrong."

Mia blows out an exaggerated breath. "Bottle your righteousness bullcrap and pitch it into the ocean."

"Doing the morally right thing is best."

"Since you're having reservations, send me the money, and I'll be sure to put it to good use at the mall."

"Mia, you're supposed to be helping me."

"It's a blessing in disguise," she says sweetly. "Would you ignore a gift from God?"

"You're playing dirty, using the phrase I've said to you on countless occasions."

"It's your choice, so do what you want, but if it were me, I wouldn't look a gift horse in the mouth."

"I'm afraid he wants something from me."

"And if he does? I say give it to him. The guy's a freaking billionaire."

"You said he's too old for me."

"Well, that was before he gave you a generous tip, and anyway, you have a crush on him."

"I never said that."

"Dominic and Pepper sitting in a tree, k-i-s-s-i-n-g. First comes love, then comes marriage, then comes the baby in the baby carriage."

"Will you stop it?"

She cackles in glee. "Fine, you big crybaby."

"You give horrible advice."

"Hey, if you listened to me more, you'd live a happier life."

"I'll sleep on it."

"Okay, on to the next topic. How was your date with string-bean man?"

"Be nice," I chide.

"Shouldn't have mentioned how skinny he is."

"It was disastrous." I go into specifics regarding the lack of chemistry and dialogue.

"Poor thing."

"We're going out again this Saturday. It'll take a miracle to get through another date."

"That sucks ass."

"What if he tries to kiss me?"

Mia makes a gagging noise. "Tell your dad to date Lester, since he likes him so much."

"Too bad he doesn't support same-sex couples," I deadpan.

"I have a surprise."

"Uh-oh."

"Hear me out."

"Go ahead."

"I'm not going to live on campus this school year."

"Why?"

"My parents finally agreed to pay half the rent for an apartment, and you're moving in."

"But my father will stop paying—"

"No buts. If he refuses to pay for classes, apply for student loans and pick up more hours at the restaurant. Also, there are a ton of scholarships you qualify for."

This is it. The moment of truth. Sweet liberation is beyond the horizon.

"Let's do it."

"That's my girl. We have two months, tops, to find a place, so we need to start searching ASAP."

"All right. You could schedule viewings for me since I work during the day, then we can narrow the list from there."

"Booyah! Party every weekend at Pepper and Mia's crib. I'll supply the drugs and you bring the alcohol, baby."

"Mia…" I warn.

"I kid. I kid."

"Yeah, right. I'm heading to bed."

"Party every other weekend?"

"Mia!"

"Okay, okay. Good night."

Mia is going to keep me on my toes, that's for sure.

Dom

Early this morning, I made a detour to Pepper's condo. After gaining entry, I installed a hidden camera in the clock hanging over the television, the ceiling fan in her bedroom, and the bathroom vent. I'll have the ability to freely watch and listen to

Pepper from any of my electronic devices. Shortly, my quarry will be successfully ensnared. A shit-eating grin adorns my face as I step off the elevator and saunter to my office. Before powering on my computer, there's a rapid tapping at the door.

"Come in."

Pepper storms in and drops the envelope on my desk. "I can't accept this."

She fidgets under my penetrating stare.

"It's a tip. Take it and be grateful."

"Ten thousand dollars is more than a tip," she says incredulously.

"I can afford it."

"What do you want?"

"You may be young, but you're not stupid." I stand, ambling around the desk and coming to a stop behind her.

Her breathing accelerates as I lean in close.

"To pop your cherry," I whisper in her ear, running the pad of my index finger over the gold cross resting above her substantial bosom. "I want to spend the summer fucking the shit out of you."

"What makes you think I'm a virgin?" she asks breathlessly.

"Innocence has a smell, and it comes off you in waves." I bury my nose in her hair, inhaling deeply. "Mouthwatering."

"Is my virginity your only motive for wanting me?"

"You're stuck as a caterpillar, but I can help transform you into a beautiful butterfly."

"Sex is meaningless without love."

"Love is an illusion," I say, kissing the nape of her neck. "Lust is so much more satisfying."

"This isn't right," she moans.

"Clear your mind and give in to your body's desire," I say, grinding my hard cock against her ass. "What will it take for me to get between your legs?"

"God, please deliver me from temptation," she implores.

"How much is your virginity worth?" I slide my hand up her bare leg, inching closer to her sweet pussy. "Another ten thousand dollars?"

Pepper swings around and slaps the fuck out of me. "I'm not for sale."

I latch on to her throat and haul her to me.

"I'll hit a woman," I growl. "It's best to remember that the next time you raise a fucking hand to me."

Pepper grasps my wrist, grappling for freedom.

"Everyone has a price, and I'll figure out yours." I fling her back. "Go."

She runs for the door, stumbling over her feet.

"Pepper."

She stops but doesn't face me.

"If you don't give me what I want, I'll take it."

She throws open the door and flees down the hall.

CHAPTER 9

Pepper

"Am I boring you, sis?" Patrick asks as he walks along beside me.

Sometimes he accompanies me on evening jaunts at a nearby park after work. Tonight, it's nice out, not too hot. The landscape is filled with cyclists, joggers, and residents enjoying the scenery. The light breeze ruffles my coily hair.

"No." I glance over at him.

"Are you sure?"

"Yes. Why?"

"Well, I've been talking to myself for the last twenty minutes," he says playfully.

"I'm sorry. I have a lot on my mind."

"You want to talk about it?" he asks.

I'm still out of sorts from the encounter with Dom earlier. My nipples peak remembering the sensation of his large hand restricting my air supply. Instead of being afraid, I inwardly pleaded for him to squeeze harder. An adrenaline rush coursed through my veins, and my center throbbed. I'm distraught I reveled in something so sadistic. Only a sick person finds pleasure in pain.

The day dragged by. I continuously looked over my shoulder while working at my cubicle, sure someone from human resources would come any second and hand me walking papers.

I shake my head. "I can handle it." Maybe if I repeat that to myself long enough, it'll come to fruition. "What were you saying?"

"Just venting about Dad." Patrick glowers. "He's a tyrant."

"School starts in two and a half months, then you'll be free of him."

"That's equivalent to a hundred years in the Russell Bryant household."

I laugh at his comparison. "I get it, trust me."

"At least next summer, I'll be on my own."

"Oh, that reminds me. I have great news."

"What?"

"Mia and I are moving in together in August."

His eyes grow big as saucers. "Seriously?"

"Yep."

"He's going to shit a brick."

"I'm scared to death."

"He knew he couldn't control us forever."

"Patrick, he did his best to raise us the right way." The need to defend him is automatic.

"He's a fraud," Patrick scoffs.

I scrunch my eyebrows. "Our father is a good man."

"He isn't. Yesterday, I discovered why he guards his cell phone like it's the Holy Grail."

"Oh, I never paid attention. What did you find?"

"I read text messages between him and Mary."

"So?"

"They're having an affair."

"That can't be true," I say in disbelief.

Our families have been connected for years, and Mary's husband, Earl, is co-pastor of the church. He and Dad met in the military and became best friends. They visited us a few times in New York over the years, and we visited them in California before relocating here, so though an affair is possible, it's highly unlikely.

"Yep, and that's not the end of it."

"What do you mean?"

"Dad is Lisa's father."

"What?" I cry, heart pounding.

Lisa is the only child of Earl and Mary.

"She's our half-sister."

"No. Our father is a God-fearing man."

My world is crashing down around me. I can't believe what I'm hearing.

"Do you honestly think he's stayed celibate all this time?"

"But he barely even talks to Mary!"

66

"Come on, Pepper. They're not going to walk around holding hands. There's a lot at stake. If this got out… Boom!"

"Lisa is nearly sixteen years old, which means he cheated on Mom. He wouldn't have done that."

"For God's sake, he's not the saint he claims to be," Patrick says, frustrated.

"It's hard for me to see him in a negative light."

"He really has you brainwashed," he snaps and walks ahead of me.

So, the shepherd is actually a wolf in disguise. This secret is big enough to divide the church and destroy everything Dad has built.

Dom

I finger my still smarting face while observing Pepper on the video feed from my computer. Her slap had strength behind it. Not a lot shocks me, but honestly, her reaction was unexpected. Pepper has more bite than I assumed, which is a pleasant surprise. But if she tries that shit again, I'll throw her over my knee and spank her ass.

Come to think of it, watching her ample ass jiggle as I deliver hit after hit is rather appealing. Maybe I should provoke her to smack me again just for that pleasure. I've been in my study since arriving home, planted in the chair at my desk, eyes fixed on the screen. She hasn't done much—ate dinner and talked to a friend on the phone. I perk up when Pepper turns off the television and heads to her bedroom where she undresses, revealing a body made for sin. I'm going to worship every fucking inch of her. Pepper deserves better than a bumbling fool for her initiation to sex.

She moves into the bathroom and switches on the shower before stepping underneath the spray of water. I lean closer to the screen in anticipation as she reaches for the washcloth and soap. Remorse at spying on Pepper during her most intimate moments eludes me. I intently follow her hand as it glides across her glistening skin. She lifts her foot to the ledge of the tub to thoroughly clean between her folds. Groaning, I adjust my stiffening dick. Goddamn, I envy that washcloth. The urge to put us both out of our misery beats at me.

"Fuck," I say, rubbing the nape of my neck.

Finally, she's done showering. The show was amazing. Shit, I'm ready to hop in my car and drive to her place for an in-person encore. Once she's back in the bedroom, she dries off and moisturizes her soft curves before putting on a T-shirt and panties. I'm disappointed she doesn't sleep in the nude, but that'll be rectified shortly.

After settling in bed, she retrieves a small black book and pen from under the mattress, then starts writing. Interesting. She has a diary. I've just been handed the keys to the castle, making a siege

68

inevitable. *What skeletons are you hiding in your closet, Pepper Bryant?* Suddenly, she hurries across the room and presses her ear to the wall.

"What the hell?" I mutter, increasing the volume on my computer.

I can't believe my ears or eyes. She's listening to her neighbors having sex.

You're a dirty girl, Pepper.

She releases a low moan as a hand disappears into her panties.

"Fucking hell." I pull my dick out, moving forward until only an inch separates my face from the monitor.

I jerk my length vigorously, imagining being inside her sweet heat. She begins violently trembling, reaching her climax at the same time my semen squirts all over the keyboard.

"Shit," I grunt.

I'm not waiting until morning to find out what secrets her diary holds. The chance of being caught is great, but it's a risk I'm willing to take. I'll make my move after she's fast asleep.

#

Dom

An hour after she dozes off, I put my plan into motion. Stealthily, I creep inside Pepper's condo and close the door quietly to avoid detection. I take the black ski mask from my pocket and pull it over my face. The adrenaline rushing through my veins serves as an aphrodisiac, increasing my need to fuck her.

I stalk towards her bedroom but don't enter. Instead, I linger in the doorway and listen to her soothing rhythmic breathing for a few moments before proceeding forward. My eyes devour her succulent form. One arm is strewn on her stomach and the other lies haphazardly next to her head. The comforter is tangled at her feet, leaving her legs slightly agape. *An invitation.* She sleeps, clueless of the danger only inches away. It would be so easy to take what I want—to pop her cherry and release the juices from her virgin cunt. She'll never know it was me.

No, that's not how I want to obtain my victory.

The need to touch her has my hand reaching out, lifting her shirt and exposing voluptuous breasts. Her eyes could pop open at any second, but I'm powerless to stop myself. I lean down and flick my tongue across her nipple until it becomes erect. Pepper turns to the side, facing me, and releases a low, tortured whimper.

I hurriedly hide beneath the bed, holding my breath.

"Dom," she whispers seductively, hardening my dick instantly.

Her low moans fill the room.

Is she dreaming of me? That thought excites me further. I roll from under the bed and climb to my knees, risking discovery, but as suspected, she remains in slumber. Pepper's hand is under the waistband of her panties, swiftly moving in her quest to find pleasure. The sight pushes me close to the edge. I watch, fascinated, and the idea of crawling between her legs flashes through my mind once more. She would be defenseless against me. It'd take little effort to pry her legs open and rip her fucking panties off. I'd use the pillow to smother her screams of pain while forcing my dick inside her tight cunt.

She wants me to fuck her. Her calling out my name is confirmation. Pepper begins to shake, attaining pleasure. Sighing blissfully, she flips onto her back. Her hand is now at her side, covered in pussy juices. Another person wouldn't tempt fate a second time, but I'm desperate for a taste. I suck on her slender fingers, stopping whenever she stirs, prepared to seek my hiding place. Pepper's savory vanilla taste explodes on my tongue. *Delicious.* Needing to come, I free my throbbing cock and plant my nose at the juncture of her thighs, drawing the smell of her into my lungs. Groaning, I begin jerking off to her appetizing scent until my seed spills onto the floor. After collecting myself, I retrieve the diary and make a hasty departure from the condo.

Soon, I'll have everything needed to bring Pepper to heel.

Pepper

Last night, I dreamed of Dom again. The heat of his breath and tongue on my nipple seemed so real. This morning I woke up drenched in sweat with his smell surrounding me. He's invading my senses.

I thought interning here was a blessing, but maybe it's leading to my ruin. Earlier, he walked by my cubicle, which is something he's never done before. I kept my eyes fixed on the computer, but I felt his gaze boring into me. My hand shook over the mouse, and the sentences on the screen became blurry. He chuckled, a low sexy sound that made my core clench. After he passed, I looked up, expecting to see his back, but he was watching me. My mouth went dry at his unnerving stare. I fled, running in the opposite direction, causing some coworkers to gawk at me.

The incident left me unsettled. Thank goodness it's lunchtime, not that I have the appetite to eat. I opted to spend the hour in the cafeteria instead of going out. I sit at the table, absentmindedly twirling the fork in my spaghetti, peering off into the distance.

"Hi."

A model-thin girl, about my height with short red hair and jade-colored eyes, stands beside me holding a tray of food.

"Hello," I reply, offering a smile.

She holds out her hand. "Trish."

"Pepper," I reply, and we shake hands.

"Awesome name."

"Thank you."

"Mind if I join you?"

"Be my guest," I answer eagerly, thrilled at the prospect of making a new friend.

"We go to the same school," Trish says, settling in the chair. "I've seen you on campus."

"Oh. You go to Duncan?"

"Yep."

I study her face, but there's no recognition. "I'm sorry. I don't remember seeing you around."

"That's not surprising, considering the sea of students on campus. I spotted you during orientation and have been meaning to introduce myself."

"I'm glad you did. We can be friends." I glance away, embarrassed for being so socially awkward. My comment was way too forward.

Idiot. She's only making polite conversation, not offering you friendship.

"That would be awesome."

"Really?" I ask excitedly.

"Of course." Trish winks at me. "I know a party happening this weekend, and you're invited."

"I've never been to one," I mumble shyly.

"Are you kidding me?"

"Nope."

"The college experience isn't complete without at least partying once."

"Maybe I'll take you up on your offer."

"I hope you do."

My life is bland, consisting of school, work, and church for the most part. It drives Mia crazy. Sure, we've gone out plenty of times, but to the movies, mall, bowling—nothing rowdy. It'd blow her mind if I broke from routine. Mia would definitely be ecstatic if I went to a party, though she'd prefer my first walk on the wild side be with her.

"What year will you be starting in the fall?" I ask.

"Senior, which means I have less than a year to get my shit together. You?"

"Junior."

"Enjoy it while you can. My mom is already hounding me about responsibility and preparing for the future."

"This experience will be a great résumé booster," I state in the hopes of putting a positive spin on her pending departure from college.

She scoffs. "I was supposed to spend the entire summer relaxing, but my godfather's girlfriend works as the administrative assistant in marketing and put in a good word for me. So, here I am. I should be sunbathing at the beach right now."

"So, you're interning in the marketing department?"

"Yes. What about you?"

"Engineering." I sip my orange soda.

"The only good thing about this place is Mr. Stone."

I start coughing, spilling my drink on the table.

"Are you okay?"

"Yes," I squawk, using napkins to clean the mess. "I drank too quickly."

"He's cute, in a dark, mysterious kind of way. Don't you think?"

"I guess so." I bite my nails, uncomfortable with the turn our conversation has taken.

"Not to mention, he's stinking rich." She sighs dreamily. "My life would be set if I bagged him."

"Oh, I... umm..."

"You look as if I chucked a box of kittens into the Pacific." She laughs. "It's just wishful thinking. He's not interested in me. I've tried flirting, showing the girls, but he doesn't give me the time of day."

"I'd better go. My break is over."

"I hope my candid nature didn't scare you off. Sometimes the signal to my brain telling my mouth to shut it isn't fast enough."

"Not at all. You remind me of my best friend, Mia." I smile fondly, thinking of Mia and her shenanigans. "She doesn't have a filter either."

"She around?" she asks, dipping a French fry in ketchup before chomping down on it.

"No. Gone for the summer."

"Lucky her. Someplace fun?"

"Just Denver."

"How very dull and boring."

"It's not so bad." I begin gathering my leftovers. "I'll be missed if I stay much longer."

"Okay, I'm due back any minute now too. Wanna swap digits before heading back to the sweatshop?"

"Sure." I store her cell number in my phone. "Catch you later."

"My mom is having minor surgery tomorrow. She'll recover in two or three days, but I took the rest of the week off to help her out."

"Oh, okay. I'll pray for her speedy recovery."

"Aww... you're adorable."

I stand, but she grasps my wrist and gives me a devilish grin. "Wear something sexy."

"I'll see."

It's time to test the waters. After all, I'm feeling a bit liberated since agreeing to move in with Mia come August, and the possibility of gaining a new friend is a plus.

CHAPTER 11

Pepper

I'm all smiles until I log in to my computer. I have an email from Dom with four words in the subject line: *Come to my office.*

My heart starts beating so fast it's bound to burst through my breastbone at any second. It's not possible to ignore or avoid him. This is his company.

What am I going to do?

Another intense confrontation with Dom will weaken my stance and draw me closer to the darkness where sin thrives. My vivid dreams of him assail me, dampening my panties.

No. I have to resist him. Hardening my resolve, I reply to his email.

Good afternoon Mr. Stone,

Consumed

I'm very busy due to a pending deadline. Is there anything I can help you with?

His response is immediate.

Get the fuck up here.

If I refuse, he'll come for me. I know it. I trudge to his office in a trance, taking the stairs in lieu of the elevator to prolong the inevitable, even if only by a couple of minutes. All too soon, I'm standing outside his lair, biting my fingernails. I rally my courage and knock.

"Come in." The deep timbre of his voice rolls over my cool skin, warming it, like the first rays of sunshine after a cold night.

I enter, finding the man haunting me reclining in his chair, his intertwined fingers resting on his stomach. I have pictured Dom lounging on a black throne, horns protruding from his scalp with brimstone and fire surrounding him. Vaguely, I hear the soft click of the door as it shuts.

"You wanted to see me," I say meekly, frozen in place.

"Have a seat."

"I can hear you from here." I remain glued to the spot.

Scowling, he storms towards me. Too paralyzed by fear, I shrink against the wall instead of running, crossing my arms above my head for protection. Flashbacks of my father's fists flying at my face transport me to the past. I scream, waiting for the blow.

Dom seizes my jaw in a painful grip.

"What the hell is the matter with you? Shut the fuck up," he whispers furiously.

"You were going to hit me," I accuse.

"I wasn't, you foolish woman, but I will if you don't obey me." He thrusts me in front of him. "Move."

I stumble forward, walking on unsteady feet. I notice two books on the gleaming wood desk, a Bible and my diary. Bile rises in my throat.

Dom's hard chest brushes against my back.

"You… you've been inside my condo," I say in a hoarse voice.

"I have." He pushes his hands under my blouse, trailing fingers up my quivering belly and kissing my neck. "Which is it going to be, salvation or damnation? Pick your poison."

"You read it?" I ask huskily, too drunk on desire to protest.

"You're a naughty girl, Pepper."

"My underwear." My eyes flutter closed. "You stole them."

"I smell them while stroking my cock." He licks the single drop of sweat trickling down my temple.

"Then I imagine bathing your beautiful chocolate face in my cum."

"What you did is illegal," I pant. "I could file a police report."

"Saying what, exactly?" He shoves his hands beneath my bra. "That I stole your book of filthy secrets? Do you want it to become public knowledge?"

If anyone else read the contents of my diary, I'd be further mortified.

"I can fulfill all of your fantasies, Pepper," he says, pinching my nipples.

"No." I whimper.

I must fight temptation.

"Your God is forgiving. He'll excuse your transgressions."

"Please… Dom… stop," I beg, my resistance waning.

"You want my mouth on your clit." His lips graze my ear as he speaks. "You pretend to be a good Christian girl, but you crave a taste of sin."

I look heavenward.

Help me.

"The devil is at your door. Will you answer?"

I recite the first Bible scripture that pops into my mind, the verses my father forced me to repeat over and over the evening he found me pleasuring myself.

"But each person is tempted when he is lured and enticed by his own desire. Then desire when it has conceived gives birth to sin and sin when it is fully grown brings forth death." I tear from his grasp and make a beeline towards safety.

"Maybe my faith isn't strong enough, because my prayers have remained unanswered."

Dom reading my most private thoughts aloud halts my retreat. He pauses briefly, then resumes airing my dirty laundry.

"My body continues to burn for Dom, day and night. I am ashamed of the things I crave for him to do. While lying in bed, my fingers venture where I long for his lips to explore. A man has never touched me there."

"No more," I beg, turning around. My diary rests in his large palm. "Have mercy on me."

"I'm not a fucking saint," he scoffs. "Your pleas won't sway me."

I could leave. He's not physically restraining me.

But I can't. My words written on paper don't hold power; they're just letters. But being spoken brings them to reality.

Dom settles back into his chair and encloses my diary in the drawer. "There's a fervor in your blood, Pepper. Suppressing it isn't going to make it disappear. Now, come sit on my desk and wrap your legs around my fucking head so I can eat."

I move towards him, unable to ignore the allure of his vulgar demand. Dom offers sustenance for my famished flesh. He clasps on to my waist, pulling me in front of him, then lifts my shirt and tongue kisses my navel. I moan, threading my fingers through his thick hair as he tugs my skirt up and drags my panties down to my ankles. Eagerly, I step out of them before being hoisted onto the desk. He grasps my knees and opens my legs wide. I bite my bottom lip self-consciously under his scrutiny.

"You don't shave?"

Humiliated, I attempt to squeeze my legs shut. No doubt he's disgusted at the unkempt state of my private area.

"Keep still," Dom growls, holding firm until I do as he instructed.

He commences his exploration, spreading my labia for a better view. "You have the plumpest clit I've ever seen."

My ragged breathing fills my ears. He grabs his cell phone and positions it at my center.

"What are you doing?" I ask anxiously, already guessing the answer but hoping I'm mistaken.

"Taking pictures."

"No!" I yell, struggling to conceal myself from his gaze once more.

He digs his strong fingers into my supple thigh so hard, surely my femur will snap in half. My eyes water. I use all my strength attempting to dislodge him, but I'm no match for his ironclad grasp.

"I'd never share them. They'll be for my own personal enjoyment." He applies more pressure, tearing a distressed cry from my throat.

"Please, let me go."

"You can make this easy or difficult. The choice is yours, but in the end, we both know I'll get what I want." He slides the phone through my quivering slit, completely covering it in my wetness.

The warm device touching my clit sends an electric pulse to my core, leaving me a trembling mess.

"Now I'll smell your sweet pussy whenever I talk on my phone."

The sight of the glistening mobile is overwhelmingly erotic.

"What's your decision?"

"Take the pictures," I answer feverishly.

"Smart girl."

He dedicates the next couple of minutes to snapping a dozen or so pictures at different angles.

"Your entrance is so damn tiny," he says gruffly. "Have you ever used a dildo or anything else?"

"N-no," I stutter.

"That's good," Dom says, pleased. "I'm going to ram my cock inside your pretty little cunt and decorate your cervix with my cum."

"I didn't agree to sex," I say in a husky voice.

He chuckles, but the sound lacks mirth.

"If I wanted this right now—" he licks around my opening— "I'd take it."

I shudder, dazed from the intimate action and the weight of his declaration.

"You see, your virginity doesn't belong to you anymore. It's my property. But because I'm a reasonable man, I'll grant you a short reprieve. And so there's no miscommunication on your part, and to make myself perfectly clear, I'm going to fuck your tight cunt and enjoy every second of stretching it the fuck out."

In the next instant, his mouth latches onto my clit, setting me on fire and disrupting my equilibrium. I release a throaty scream and fall back onto the desk, knocking his computer to the floor in my wild state. His rapidly moving tongue flicks back and forth, increasing the ferocity of the blaze. How can my Lord and Savior be opposed to something this amazing? The burning spreads, growing hotter and hotter to pool at my center. I thrash uncontrollably, unable to cease my wayward body. It's coming. The inferno is nearing its peak—

"What the fuck is going on in here?" a man bellows.

I crane my neck and see two men standing in the middle of the room. The older man is dressed in an impeccable suit, similar to Dom's. They're almost the spitting image of each other, but his blond hair is a bit lighter, and he has a beard. He pins me with a death glare. The younger guy has a carefree aura about him, unlike the other gentleman who oozes a no-nonsense demeanor, reminding me of my father. His mop of curls matches twinkling brown eyes. He's attired more casually in a hoodie and jeans. His lips pinch together, forming a thin line in an effort to contain laughter. I sit up and try to break away from Dom, but he won't relinquish his grip on my thighs. I've never been so humiliated in my entire life.

"Go away, goddamn it. I'm busy," he snarls.

I grab the file by my hip to protect my modesty since I'm on full display for these strange men to see. My vaginal fluids cover the lower half of Dom's face, the evidence of our carnal activity glistening like diamonds. Even worse is the lone pubic hair attached to his top lip.

"Are you fucking kidding?" no-nonsense man snaps.

"Get the fuck out of here, Jensen!" he shouts. "And take Drew with you!"

Drew erupts into guffaws, losing the battle to keep his amusement at bay. "I'm sorry, but this is a classic moment."

"Bringing a skank to your place of business is probably the dumbest thing you've ever done," Jensen chides.

"Jesus, I'm not a damn child."

"Your misconduct says otherwise," Jensen counters.

"She's an intern here."

"Oh, well, then it's perfectly okay," he replies sarcastically.

I make a stressed, mewling noise. I'd be grateful if I vanished into a black hole right now.

"Spare me your fucking high-and-mighty attitude," Dom says in irritation.

Jensen gives me a dirty look. "How old are you?"

"I'm—"

Dom cuts off my reply. "She's legal."

"How legal? She barely looks eighteen."

"People will start to wonder where I am," I say, hoping to end this compromising situation.

I breathe a sigh of relief when he lets me go, and I immediately jump to my feet.

"Nice ass." Drew smirks.

"You're asking for a beating," Dom threatens.

I hurriedly make myself decent and bend down to retrieve my panties from the floor, but Dom snatches them up.

"I need those."

"These are mine," he says, moving to his feet.

The man already has at least six pairs, but now is not the time to argue. I cut my losses and hightail it out of there.

"Don't go far, Pepper. The appetizer was delicious, but the entrée is going to be orgasmic." I hear him call behind me.

I dash to the stairwell and race down the stairs. My coworkers gape at me when I burst through the door and frantically race towards my cubicle.

Lloyd steps out of his office, directly in my path. He grasps my shoulders, preventing me from barreling into him. "Pepper, are you okay?"

"Umm… I'm not feeling too well," I answer breathlessly.

"Take the rest of the day off."

"Thank you."

Dom

"You two better have a damn good reason for being here," I say, annoyed at their interruption.

"Do you mind cleaning your face?" Jensen asks in disgust. "I can't have a conversation with you looking like that."

I take the handkerchief from my breast pocket and wipe my mouth. "Happy?"

"Anyone could've walked in and witnessed your unethical behavior," Jensen chastises.

"No one in this building is brave enough to waltz into my office without permission." I saunter around the desk.

"You're going to start a shitstorm," he warns.

"You think?" Drew says, flopping into the chair, overcome with another shriek of laughter.

"Give your caterwauling a goddamn rest," I bark, glaring at my younger brother.

"Well, man, this shit is hilarious."

I punch him in the chest, resorting to physical violence to shut him up—the same tactic used when he got on my nerves as children. The only difference is, he doesn't run crying to our mother for refuge anymore. He's six years younger than me. Drew dropped out of college during his sophomore year. He was supposed to follow in Jensen's footsteps and become a lawyer but chose to pursue a music career instead. Now he's an award-winning singer and songwriter.

The three of us couldn't be more different. Jensen is stern and serious. He has a stick so far stuck up his ass it's practically protruding from his skull. Drew, on the other hand, is a jokester and life of the party. He never takes anything seriously. Me, well, I'm the bad-tempered asshole.

"Hey, that hurt, man," he whines.

I'd love to smash Jensen's face in, but we both wound up in the hospital seeking medical attention after our last altercation. He was twenty-three at the time, and I was eighteen. Dad was a boxer in high school and believed our disputes should be settled with fists, but our mother made us promise never to fight again.

"Starting a relationship with an intern is a conflict of interest," Jensen cuts in.

"Who said anything about a relationship?"

"So you plan to use that poor girl?" he sputters.

"For God's sake, Jensen, spare me your moral tirade!" I bellow. "I don't want to fucking hear it!"

"Soooo," Drew drawls. "She's a cutie. Does she have any sisters or maybe cousins, perhaps?"

"No," I deadpan. "If you two aren't here for any other reason than to piss me off, you'll have to excuse me."

"This is an intervention," Jensen announces, crossing his arms.

"Is that so?" I arch an eyebrow.

"We're going to Dad and Mom's for dinner on Sunday, and you're coming." Drew stretches out his legs.

"And if I refuse?"

"Don't be a dick. They hardly ever see you," Drew says.

"I visited them two weeks ago."

"You stopping by for ten minutes after work isn't exactly visiting," Jensen scoffs. "Please, for our mother."

"I'll be there," I sullenly agree.

"One more thing," Jensen says.

"What now?" I want them gone ASAP so I can go in search of Pepper.

"I'm planning a weekend getaway for brotherly bonding at Lake Arrowhead."

"I won't be available."

"How do you know? I didn't mention a date," Jensen counters.

"Come on, we haven't been to the cabin together in ages. It'll be fun. We can do a little fishing and swimming," Drew says.

I have plenty of good memories there of drunken nights filled with good food. "I could rearrange my schedule."

"Great, I'll plan for the second weekend in July," Jensen states.

"Fine. Now if you don't mind, I have a very important business matter to attend to."

"Business?" Jensen snorts.

Drew starts that damn laughing again. "Does your pressing engagement include a sexy intern with a shapely derriere and huge boobs?"

I stalk over to him to deliver another blow, but he gets up and bolts out the door. "Meet you at the car, Jensen," he yells.

"You've always been a jerk, even as a kid, for some unexplained reason. Truth be told, you were that way from birth, ruining the whole nurture versus nature argument. I threw you in the garbage can when you were a baby, determined to get rid of you." He chuckles. "Mom found you screaming at the top of your lungs. Boy was she livid, but not as much as me when she took you out. I pleaded with her to put you back."

"There you have it. I was destined to be a schmuck."

"The older you got, the worse your attitude became, and then after Lauren—"

"Do you enjoy pissing me off?"

"Just wondering when your vendetta against the world will end."

"I'll see you on Sunday."

"Bringing that girl into your sordid universe is selfish. She'll get lost in the darkness."

"Too late. She already accepted the first-class ticket, and I have a no-refund policy. It's not my fault if she didn't read the fine print," I respond, exiting my office.

Pepper passed the point of no return the moment I laid my eyes on her. Call me a monster, hurl every bad name at me in existence, I couldn't care less. Nothing is going to stop me from fucking her.

Pepper's cubicle is empty. Despite the curious glances, I hover for five minutes before proceeding to Lloyd's office. I stand in the open doorway.

"Where's Pepper?"

He peers up from his task. "She's ill, so I gave her permission to go home."

"How long has she been gone?"

"I'd say twenty minutes. Is there something wrong?"

"No."

He regards me strangely, undoubtedly finding my inquiry odd. I've never shown interest in a specific intern in the past.

I pivot on my heel and head back upstairs. Pepper will soon discover she's a mouse trapped in a maze, and each endeavor towards freedom only leads to a dead end.

Pepper

I showered after arriving home, then hid under my comforter. I'm staying in bed for the rest of the evening. I'm a horrible person. I let my infatuation with Dom cloud my better judgment. How can I step foot inside Stone Incorporated again? It's too late to apply for a summer internship anywhere else. I'll tell him it was a mistake and can't be repeated. He'll have to understand and respect my decision. So much was happening, I completely forgot he broke into my condo and rummaged through my personal belongings and dirty laundry. My face heats in horror at that thought. It's time for girl talk. I grab my cell off the nightstand and ring Mia.

"Hello," she answers groggily.

"I did something really bad."

"You forgetting a Bible verse is not the end of the world," she deadpans.

"Ha ha, very hilarious, but that's not why I called."

"What then? Did you finally kick your father in the balls?" she asks, yawning.

"Were you sleeping?"

"Yep."

"It's not like you to take a nap at this hour."

"I've been asleep all day."

"But it's almost five!" I exclaim.

"I went to a rave last night and didn't get in until six."

"For shame, Mia—"

"Oh, hush, you remind me of Grandmother," she grumbles. "Spill the tea."

"I... at work... umm—"

"Pepper," Mia says, exasperated. "Collect yourself and tell me what the hell happened."

"I had oral sex."

"You sucked dick!" she yells, now wide awake at my confession.

"No, he did it to me."

"Who?"

"Dom."

"What the fuck?" she screams, then howls in laughter.

"This isn't funny!"

"Oh, yeah, it is."

"What am I going to do?"

"How was it?"

"It was… it was… incredible."

"Did you orgasm?"

"No."

"Evidently it wasn't that great," she scoffs.

"We were interrupted."

"By who?"

"I don't know. Two men barged into his office."

"Whoa, pump the brakes. He ate your pussy in his office?"

"Yes."

"Where?"

"On his desk."

"Holy moly," she says in amazement. "I'm so proud of you."

"This news hardly qualifies for accolades." I roll to my side.

"It does in my book."

"I've made a mess of things."

"There's nothing wrong with engaging in a summer fling."

"Mia, I'm not interested in meaningless intercourse."

"Did you just say intercourse? Having *sex* is not a crime."

"I'm not a good Christian," I groan, throwing my arm across my forehead.

"Ugh!" Mia screeches. "You're giving me a headache."

"He has my diary."

"How the hell did he get it?"

"He broke into my condo."

"Well, shit, that's romantic and stalkerish as fuck at the same time."

"He stole my dirty underwear too."

"Come again," she says slowly.

I recount my search for the missing garments and Dom's subsequent admission of his involvement in their disappearance.

"Okay, that's super freaking weird. Why did he take them? God, maybe he wears women's panties."

"He said..." I clear my throat. "He said... he smells them... umm... while he's pleasuring himself."

"I'm disgusted and a little intrigued. It's quite common for rich people to be eccentric."

"I'm scared—"

"Why? Did he hurt you? I'll hop on the first available flight to California and go apeshit on his ass."

"No, I'm afraid because he's not going to stop and—"

"No means no. If he continues to sexually harass you, sue his ass."

"You don't get it."

"Explain it to me."

"I want him." I pause. "A lot."

"Heck, girlie, go get you some billionaire ding-a-ling."

I squeal, startled, when Dom appears in the doorway.

"What's going on?" Mia asks in alarm.

He saunters into my bedroom, as if he has every right to be here. "What part of *don't go far* didn't you fucking understand?"

I'm too speechless to respond. He plucks my cell from my hand and ends the call. It starts ringing immediately.

"Take off your clothes and lie on the bed," he says, switching my phone to silent mode before placing it on the nightstand.

I'm too shocked to move. Growling in irritation, he roughly yanks me to my feet.

"You're testing my patience," he snarls. "I expect immediate obedience. Remove your clothes, or I'll rip them off you."

I shake my head. "Submit yourselves therefore to God. Resist the devil, and he will flee from you."

His sinister laughter sends chills racing along my flesh. "Does it look like I'm *fleeing*? You'll worship me as your God by the time I'm done with you." He clasps my hair in an excruciating grip and bites down on my earlobe.

I wince in pain and struggle to break loose. Dom forces me onto the bed and climbs on top of me. I fight in earnest, though my efforts prove useless. In mere seconds, my T-shirt and panties lie in tatters on the floor.

"I'll have to make you hurt if you don't behave."

My fist connects with his jaw. In retaliation, he slaps me across the cheek. The right side of my face explodes in agony, momentarily disorienting me. A tangy taste fills my mouth. His hand encircles my neck, constricting my breathing.

"You were warned never to hit me again."

I try to pry his fingers away, but his hold remains steadfast. I'm swiftly losing the battle to stay conscious.

"Seeing you bleed makes my cock hard." An evil gleam lights up his amber eyes. "I could've fractured your skull but held back. You should be thankful."

A loud knock sounds at the door.

He releases my throat. "Who the fuck are you expecting?"

"Nobody," I wheeze, barely able to talk.

The knocking turns into banging.

"Don't move." He leaves the room and returns within seconds. "It's the police. Put on your robe and tell them everything is fine."

"Okay."

This is my chance to seek help. I'd hate for Dom to get arrested, but he scares me more than my father. I never thought anyone would ever accomplish that feat. He has no qualms about hurting me. In fact, he seems to find pleasure in it, but I still crave him. His unapologetic attitude excites me, overshadowing my self-preservation. Dom takes whatever he deems his and doesn't fear consequences. He makes me covet my own destruction.

"I'll ruin your career and bankrupt your father if you say one word."

I study his face and come to the conclusion he's dead serious.

"Don't invite them in."

I nod and head into the bathroom to get my robe. After covering myself, I make my way to the front door. I peer through the peephole and spot two police officers, one male and the other female.

"Can I help you?"

"Pepper Bryant?" the female officer asks.

"Yes."

"Your friend, Mia, called the police and requested a welfare check on you."

"I'm fine."

"Please open the door, ma'am," she says.

I concede, knowing the officers won't leave unless they visually verify I'm unharmed.

"I appreciate you both coming, but as you can see, I'm perfectly fine."

"Your friend said she heard you scream, then the call disconnected."

"I saw a mouse and overreacted." I laugh.

The female officer eyes me suspiciously while her partner seems bored. "Your face is swollen."

"I bumped into the wall trying to outrun the mouse."

"Deena, she's good. Let's go," the male officer says and marches down the hall.

"Enjoy the rest of your evening, ma'am."

"You too."

Once again, I'm left at the mercy of the beast. If I were honest, I'd admit it's exactly where I desire to be, but denial is my lifeline. Holding on to it prevents me from being battered in the tornado that is Dominic Stone.

"Pepper," he says huskily. "I'm waiting."

I hurriedly walk towards my bedroom but notice Dom sitting on the toilet and change directions. He maneuvers me between his legs and unties my robe. The fluffy material parts, revealing my nakedness. His pursual of my body scorches me to the marrow. He trails his fingers through the downy hair at the crux of my thighs.

"This is interfering with my meal," he says, guiding my foot to the edge of the bathtub. "You're due for a shave."

"I can do it on my own," I reply timidly.

"I'm sure you can." He turns the faucet on and holds his hand beneath the stream of water. "But I insist."

His eyes bore into mine while he thoroughly wets my folds, then picks up the can of shaving cream lying next to my razor on the sink. He commences shearing my tuft of curls. I'm a bit jumpy having a sharp blade near my private area, but Dom is

102

meticulous and doesn't rush. My trepidation fades as he completes the task with expert precision.

"All done." He smacks my butt and stands. "Keep your pussy bald."

"This is dangerous," I whisper.

Soon we'll pass the point of no return, then my world will cave in on me. Dom lives by his own rules, so he'll persevere, but me… I'll be buried in the rubble, suffocating until I'm no more.

"Danger can be the perfect aphrodisiac if wielded properly." His voice is silk, hitting me like a bolt of lightning and fraying already raw nerves.

"Have you no common decency?"

"Fuck no. No remorse, pity, or sympathy either, and I go to sleep at night with a clear conscience. I relish using your weakness to my advantage." He slides his thumb over my lips. "Your surrender is certain."

"What makes you so sure?"

"Pepper, I've read your dreams." He kisses my forehead. "You lust for domination, and I'm the man who'll fulfill your fantasies. All you have to do is be my slut."

"You know my darkest secrets, but you've yet to share yours."

"I have none."

"Are you telling the truth?"

"My life isn't your fucking business. Now wash up and bring your ass into the bedroom." Dom exits the bathroom.

I finish my bird bath in a matter of minutes and go to my bedroom. Dom sits propped on the mountain of pillows decorating my bed, his hands behind his head and his ankles crossed. He's obviously right at home. His shoes are arranged neatly against the wall. This could be the day I lose my virginity. Am I prepared for the consequences? If I cross this bridge, there'll be no turning back.

"Remove your robe."

My aching jaw is a reminder of the ramifications if I defy him. It's not wise to poke the bear again, so I err on the side of caution. The fuzzy cotton cascades down my arms and pools at my feet. He's seen all of me, but it's difficult to abandon modesty. I cover my breasts and the juncture of my thighs.

Dom frowns slightly. "Bare yourself to me."

Reluctantly, I acquiescence to his command. His fervent gaze lovingly feasts on my heated skin. I'm in awe watching the crotch of his pants extend, forming a large tent. The suspense is overpowering, nearly reducing me to madness. I hyperventilate, consumed by arousal and the staggering hunger he causes in me.

"Perfection." His gruff tone effectively pebbles my nipples despite the lack of direct contact. "Turn around, slowly."

I tremble under Dom's intense inspection.

"Stop," he demands. "Your impeccable ass is s work of art. Come to me."

I crawl onto my bed and spot the bottle of chocolate syrup I use for ice cream sundaes next to Dom. I give him a cursory look, wondering why he took it from the refrigerator.

He shoves me backwards and settles his broad shoulders between my legs. Both thighs are treated to gentle kisses before he squeezes the flavorful condiment onto my flushed mound. The cold sauce trickles to my anus. He grasps my knees and spreads me open, lifting my bottom off the mattress. I'm fully exposed at this angle. Dom's talented tongue laves every square inch of my vulva, then travels downwards to my puckered hole and continues his unrelenting assault. The intimacy of the act transports me to another level of consciousness. Only a single hit of Dom and I'm intoxicated—utterly addicted. My dreams and reality combine, making it impossible to separate one from the other. I twist my hands in the sheets, frightened, needing to grab ahold of something tangible to prevent myself from disintegrating due to sensory overload. He latches on to my clit and my back arches. I'm suspended in time, floating in darkness, then I fall for what seems an eternity. Suddenly, the ground appears, but it's too late to brace for impact, so I accept my fate. The crash is brutal. I explode, burning in a smoldering blaze that chars me to the bone. I bolt upright, screaming so loud and long I'm amazed every glass in my condo doesn't shatter.

I sob uncontrollably, and Dom embraces me. He took me straight to Hell, and the visit was heavenly.

"Crying is pointless. Save your tears for when I fuck you," he murmurs. "Now, dry your face and suck my cock."

Dom frees his rigid shaft.

"Please go." I have to pray and ask for forgiveness.

"I prefer to be inside you, but I promised you a reprieve, and I'm a man of my word. You're going to deepthroat my cock and be grateful your virginity will be intact come morning."

"I can't," I weep.

Dom clutches the scruff of my neck and guides me towards his manhood. "Open."

I comply, and he drives his erection to my tonsils, gagging me. His massive girth blocks my airway. Panicking, I squirm earnestly to get away, or risk being suffocated to death. His grip on my nape tightens painfully, rendering me immobile.

"Breathe through your fucking nose and watch your goddamn teeth."

He savagely plunges upwards at warp speed, not giving me a moment to adjust to his violent invasion.

"Wider," he shouts.

Snot flows from my nostrils and saliva drips onto his testicles. I vomit a little, powerless to keep the contents of my stomach at bay. At the same instant, I lose control of my bladder and urinate on my bedding. He emits a guttural noise, and his salty flavor invades my taste buds.

"Swallow every last drop," he rasps, grinding his hips against my face.

Finally, he pulls his length out of my mouth, and I greedily draw in lifesaving oxygen.

"Come to my office during your lunch hour tomorrow," he says, wiping himself clean on my pillowcase.

Dom rights his clothes and dons his shoes, then strolls out of my bedroom. Though he left me crippled, in a near catatonic state and covered in my own bodily fluids, I yearn for more. I'm undeniably demented for enjoying his brutality. I toe the line of perdition and the promised land. The former leads to the netherworld, and the latter, everlasting glory. I hesitate at the fork in the road even knowing which path to journey. Hell beckons, and it's too tantalizing to ignore.

CHAPTER 14

Dom

At noon, Pepper walks into my office. I left the door ajar for her but was prepared to drag her ass in here caveman style if she didn't show. Fuck the wagging tongues and speculations. A short-sleeved magenta blouse hugs her bountiful chest and heather-gray pants showcase her scrumptious thighs. Pepper's signature flat black shoes grace her feet. She would look magnificent in a pair of designer high heels. The sunlight brightens her flawless mahogany skin. She's a fucking queen and deserves a crown embellished in diamonds adorning her lustrous curls. I recline in my plush leather chair and loosen the top button of my dress shirt. She licks her plump lips as she tracks my hand, beckoning me silently.

"Ready for lesson two?"

"Yes," she answers, staring directly into my eyes.

Interesting. That's new, she usually eludes my gaze. Where's my demure girl?

I saunter up to her and offer my hand, curious to see if she accepts without hesitation. She does. My angel is full of surprises today. I escort her to the spacious dwelling attached to my office.

"Wow, I assumed this door led to a closet or bathroom," she says in amazement. "It's triple the size of my condo."

I tug her to the bed and guide her to sit on the edge of it. "Undress me."

"What?" she squeaks.

"Ahh, there's my shy girl."

Pepper's alluring big doe orbs peer up at me. Her innocence is so fucking seductive. I caress her exquisite face, and she rubs her silken skin against my palm—a kitten eager for her master's affections. If I had any integrity, I'd send her packing, but my heart is made of *Stone*. I'm a fucking parasite, and I plan to feed on her until she's drained dry.

"Explore my body, uninhibited. I failed to grant you the chance yesterday."

Pepper removes my crisp white Brioni shirt with unsteady hands, then examines every ridge of my rock-solid chest, paying special homage to the distinct V descending into my pants. She makes quick work of my belt buckle as her bashfulness evaporates and she becomes bolder. Minutes later, I'm completely disrobed, giving her access to view me in the buff. My long erection juts out proudly, slightly curving to the left. Her mouth is only a hairsbreadth from the thick mushroom-shaped head. Each exhale of her breath glides across my throbbing shaft, mirroring a lover's tender touch. She peruses it in wonderment.

"Touch it," I demand huskily.

Pepper slides her thumb along my slit, smearing pre-cum over my sensitive glans. A low, tortured groan reverberates from the pit of my stomach.

"Did I hurt you?" she asks, nibbling her lip nervously. "I'm sorry."

"No. It felt fucking amazing. Continue."

Encouraged, Pepper restarts her inspection, delicately tracing the veins on my cock. It takes considerable restraint not to claim her chastity like a marauding Viking on a quest to pillage. Next, she ventures lower and cups my scrotum.

"Goddamn," I growl.

"They're so heavy."

"Suck them."

She eagerly twirls her tongue around my ball sac before surprisingly engulfing both into her wet haven.

"Fuck."

She greedily draws on my testicles, creating an unbreakable suction. Shit, I'll unload if she keeps this up.

"Enough," I say, dislodging her.

"More."

"No need to worry, I'm just getting started." I pull Pepper to her feet and strip her bare. "Spit on my dick and make it sloppy."

She drops to her knees and saturates my shaft in saliva until it's dripping.

"Good, now lie down on the bed."

She hastily does as I instruct.

I climb up her body and kneel below her voluptuous tits.

"Have you ever heard of mammary intercourse?" I ask, fondling her nipples to hard points.

"No," she says, shaking her head.

"It's a form of masturbation using breasts."

"How?"

"Let me enlighten you. Firmly press your breasts together."

"Like this?" she asks, squeezing the sizeable mounds together.

"Yes, good girl."

I push my length between her ample bosoms, and the supple flesh succumbs to my intrusion, enclosing me in a sweltering paradise. I worship her nipples, pinching and plucking the hard pearls while plowing into the compact space above her breastbone. She moans and bites her bottom lip.

"Your areoles are the prettiest shade of brown."

Pepper struggles to maintain the grip on her breasts through my brutal strokes.

"Hold them tighter."

After a few more thrusts, she cries out, orgasming at the same time I ejaculate on her neck and chin.

"How was that possible?" Pepper asks, bewildered.

"Not many women can climax from breast stimulation, but yours are extremely sensitive."

"I had no idea an orgasm could happen that way."

"With me, the sky is the limit," I say, massaging my semen into her skin, thoroughly marking my territory.

"Don't move." I amble to the refrigerator and grab a cucumber.

Pepper eyes my hand warily as I approach her. "Plan on making a salad?"

"Among other things."

"What do you mean?"

"A juicy steak and salad sound delicious for lunch." I lie next to her. "But there's a special flavor I want to add to it."

"What flavor?"

"Pussy." I move down her body and position the cucumber at her opening.

"No!" Pepper shouts. "This isn't how I want to lose my virginity."

"Shh… you're upsetting yourself for no reason. My dick will have the pleasure of rupturing your hymen. I'm only putting the tip in."

Slowly, I insert the cucumber into her tight sheath and stare, enamored by the expanding of her pink muscles. I halt the invasion about an inch in and lean closer to study the marvelous sight.

"This is the most beautiful fucking thing I've ever seen in my life."

My tongue briskly lashes her nub while I fuck her with the vegetable in short, controlled strokes, careful not to penetrate too deeply. She tries to twist away, but I wrap my left arm around her thigh, halting her progress.

"Dom, please! It's too much!" she cries, peaking as spasms contort her body.

A cream and liquid secretion flows from her fluttering pussy.

"Divine," I murmur, coating the cucumber in her delectable nectar and giving it to Pepper. "Prepare our lunch. Two steaks and ingredients to mix a salad are in the fridge."

"Okay." She moves to unstable legs and collects her clothing from the floor.

"Leave them off."

She balks but drops the garments on the bed.

"Rare and bloody for me," I say.

She nods in acknowledgment. "I have to use the bathroom first."

"Hurry," I gripe "I'm hungry."

"Bossy," she mumbles, disappearing into the bathroom.

"Damn right," I call after her. "It'll be better for you to remember that."

A couple minutes later she emerges. "There's no mirror."

"If you had this face, you would avoid looking at your reflection too."

"You're still alive, and that's what counts."

"I beg to differ," I say caustically.

"You're not as hideous as you think."

"My money is what women find attractive."

"Not me."

There's such sincerity in her statement I almost believe her, but I'm no idiot. Women are treacherous, skilled in the power of seduction. A characteristic ingrained in their chromosomes at the time of conception. I will never allow a woman to play me again, especially not a twenty-year-old virgin. It'd be a cold day in Hell.

"Stop talking and cook my damn food."

"I don't appreciate how you speak to me," she says in a cracked voice, unsure if she should defend herself but stands her ground nonetheless.

"Your virgin blood will be smeared on my dick in the next thirty seconds if you don't shut the fuck up."

She audibly gulps and hightails it to the kitchen. I avidly observe her from the bed as she sautés the ribeye in olive oil, butter, garlic, salt, pepper, and thyme, then chops the vegetables and other fixings for the tossed salad. Her shapely legs are fucking fantastic. And that ass, my God, it is exemplary. I should be jailed for the wicked things I intend to do to her. Pepper sets the table diligently.

"Lunch is ready," she announces. "Can I get dressed now?"

"No."

"I'm not comfortable eating naked."

"Then watch me eat." I stroll to the sink and wash my hands.

"What will you do if I disobey?"

"Do you think it's wise to challenge me?" I ask menacingly, sitting at the table. "Go ahead, test the waters."

Following a second or two of indecision, she opts to sit at the table. Good, because I'm hungry and not in the mood to whop her ass.

"The food looks great."

"Thank you," she replies grudgingly.

I pick up the fork and knife.

"Wait, we have to say a prayer."

"I don't pray, but go for it while I enjoy my meal."

She clasps her hands together and says a short prayer.

I smirk, noticing a particular vegetable absent from her salad. "No cucumbers?"

"I didn't want any," she says in a high-pitched voice.

"Why is that?"

"You covered it in my... in my... vaginal fluids."

"You're going to suck your juices off my dick plenty, so get used to the taste." I give her some cucumbers off my plate. "Bon appétit."

She pours vinaigrette on her leafy greens and begins to eat tentatively.

"Why were you homeschooled?" I ask, cutting into the juicy meat.

"My father thought it best," she answers evasively.

"Explain."

"He didn't want my behavior influenced by peers."

"Your unconventional childhood must've been hard on you."

"It doesn't surprise me you know details of my life since you love invading my privacy. My upbringing wasn't a happy one and very strict."

Her haunted eyes pierce my hard heart. Fuck, she's getting to me.

"Did he hurt you?" I'll decapitate that motherfucker.

"I prefer not to have this discussion, please."

"I'll drop it for now since you said please, but we will finish this."

We resume our meal in relative silence, but I sense she's distracted.

"Do you have something to say?"

"What you did was unnatural."

"But you enjoyed it," I state matter-of-factly.

She averts her gaze, shamefaced.

"There isn't too much off-limits for me in regards to fucking. I'm fond of experimenting. What others find taboo, I call an acquired taste. Sex for me is more than attaining climax, it's a pilgrimage. Orgasms are a dime a dozen and forgotten the moment culmination recedes. Lewd, obscene fucking is my specialty. I'll give you sex that's so raunchy and disgusting you'll need to bathe in holy water afterwards."

"And when the journey ends?"

"We disembark, separately."

"Is it always so simple for you?"

"It's best to steer clear of complications."

"W-we could f-fall in love," she stutters.

This line of conversation is dangerous.

"Haven't you been listening?" I ask, annoyed.

"Love is real."

"Not between a man and a woman. It's conditional, therefore an illusion."

"That's not true."

"How would you know? You've never even had a boyfriend."

"Everyone has a soul mate."

I remember being young, dumb, and optimistic, until reality shot me in the fucking heart.

"You're naïve."

"Have you ever been in love?"

"I thought so once, long ago."

"What happened?"

"I discovered she was a conniving bitch."

"Were you married?"

"Engaged. It's fortunate I learned of her true objective before the wedding day."

"Which you believe was monetary gain?"

"There's no question that was her motivation."

"Is she the reason why you're this way?"

"And how am I exactly?" I ask irritably.

"You're hurting."

"No, I was fucking enraged, but I'm not anymore."

"You are. You're letting whatever occurred in the past prevent you from happiness."

"Don't think for a second you're the beauty that can tame the beast," I snarl.

"I'm just trying to understand you."

"Wake the fuck up, Pepper," I sneer. "This is a summer fling and nothing more. Don't fancy yourself falling in love with me, or you'll be the one who gets hurt. Finish your food and get back to work."

Goddamn, it never fails. I haven't met a woman yet who hasn't tried to *fix* me.

CHAPTER 15

Pepper

I haven't seen Dom since Tuesday. Maybe I should count myself lucky. I've prayed to my heavenly father, asking for the fortitude to reject temptation, because I'm not able to deny *him*. But it's Dom who's ignoring me. I upset him during our last conversation. It seems love and his ex-fiancée are forbidden topics. I went to his office every day at noon and found the door locked. I'm pathetic. He's left me enthralled, captivated, and ready for another sojourn to the bowels of Satan's dungeon. Had I been strong enough to revolt against my unholy compulsion, I would be blissfully ignorant to the pleasures of the flesh. How am I supposed to forget the fire he stoked within me? My work has suffered; it's impossible to focus. I spent most of the time glancing around whenever I heard a door open or footsteps, hoping to catch a glimpse of my tormentor, the devil incarnate, but I never saw him. His daily walks past my cubicle stopped. My nights have been unbearable, consisting of sweaty limbs, tangled sheets, and passion-filled dreams. He texted me his cell phone number the day he reduced me to a puddle in my condo. I've typed out several messages only to delete them. I decided to take the high road, though I prefer not to. Mia said I should forget about him, and that's putting it mildly. She used more colorful terms. I described to her the chocolate syrup and cucumber incidents in detail. She wasn't outraged on my behalf but envious and vowed to spice up her sex life.

The workweek went downhill from there, concluding with another tortuous evening in Lester's company on Friday. I can't pretend anymore. There's absolutely no way I'll ever entertain a relationship with him. He took it to the next level by holding my hand like we were a happy couple. His touch was beyond uncomfortable and made my skin crawl. And the white foam forming at the corners of his thin lips made me queasy. The last straw was his attempt to give me a goodnight kiss, which I promptly evaded. I'm prepared for my father's wrath. Continuing this farce is unfair to Lester and me, but I'm waiting on the right moment to tell him. It's a delicate situation due to Dad's and Lester's friendship. I have to broach the subject very carefully.

The only bright side to my less than stellar week is Trish. She'll be here at any moment to pick me up for the party. I've been pacing my living room for the last several minutes. I'm so nervous I could vomit. I took a trip to a popular clothing store earlier, and with Mia guiding me on video chat, purchased a figure-hugging spaghetti strap royal blue dress. It's knee-length and shows a little cleavage. It's modest compared to the other dresses I saw but still the most revealing outfit in my wardrobe. I treated myself to new shoes too, not the usual frumpy grandma type either. I elected to be daring and bought my first pair of pumps. Initially, I selected black, but Mia scolded me and accused me of being dull. She spoke the truth. Every single pair I own are either black, brown, or beige. I chose shiny, metallic silver high heels, and I'm glad I did. I finally replaced my stolen underwear too. After arriving home, I washed my unruly hair, then applied a generous amount of curling custard to tame it. The soft, bouncy curls dance around my face as I wear a hole in my carpet. My face is void of any makeup since I'm clueless on how to apply the stuff, but I did cover my lips in clear gloss. My cell phone rings, and I run to the table where I left it to answer the call.

"Hello."

"Are you ready to party?" Trish shouts.

"Yep." I laugh.

"Then come on out. Your carriage awaits you."

"Coming," I say excitedly.

Almost an hour later, Trish stops at the entrance of a gated community. A security guard sits inside a booth.

"Hello, can I help you ladies?" he asks.

"We were invited to a party." Trish rattles off the address, and we hand over our driver's licenses.

He peers at a list attached to a clipboard for confirmation.

"Okay, you're both good to go." He presses a button, and the electronic gate slides open, granting us entry.

"I've never seen him before, must be new. He's a cutie." She pops her candy apple red lips. "Maybe I'll bring him a drink later."

"I doubt if he's allowed to consume alcohol while working."

"One drink won't hurt."

Big houses, manicured lawns, and expensive looking cars in driveways greet us. It's plain to see the residents who live here are well off. Not on the same financial plane as Dom, but they have to be earning at least six figures annually.

"Wow, this is a really nice neighborhood."

"Did you think the party would be in the ghetto?" she asks, parallel parking.

"Of course not," I say quickly. "I didn't mean it that way."

"Chill, it's no biggie." She eyes me speculatively while tapping her index finger on her chin.

Trish is the epitome of fashion. Her gold sequin dress is so short her panties are visible. She styled her mass of red hair in a messy bun, and her makeup is expertly applied.

"What?"

"You look kind of drab, but I've got you covered." She grabs her purse from the back seat. "It's a good thing I packed my emergency makeup pouch."

Trish works her magic with keen attentiveness.

"Done." She grins, handing me a small rectangular mirror. "Take a look."

I'm speechless. Trish did an amazing job. The dark smoky eyeshadow brings out the color of my eyes, and a touch of blush graces my symmetrical cheekbones. A thick coat of mascara extends my eyelashes, and my lips now match hers.

"Thank you so much."

"No problem. Let's go."

We traipse alongside each other up the long cobblestone driveway already lined with dozens of cars towards the brick dwelling. The drum of music becomes louder as we draw closer.

"We're going to be the baddest bitches at the party," she says confidently, opening the unlocked door.

I'm floored by the sight before me. A disc jockey is stationed at the back wall, and a strobe light affixed on the arched ceiling washes the room in bright colors. This puts me in the mind of the clubs I've seen depicted in numerous movies. It's really crowded. There must be a hundred people in here, possibly more.

"Pepper." Camden appears at my side. "Welcome to my humble abode."

"This party is epic," Trish says.

"This is your house?" I ask incredulously.

"Nah, my parents', but they're in Paris for the summer."

"Wait a minute. Do you two know each other?" I ask.

"Nope, it's a small world," he answers. "And anyway, I don't recognize half the people here."

"Let's dance." Trish takes my hand and ushers me through the throng of gyrating bodies.

"I don't know how to."

"That's cool, just follow my lead."

She twirls around to face me and begins to provocatively sway her hips. I try to mimic her movements, but I'm too awkward and uncoordinated to be successful. Someone clasps my waist from behind and grinds against my bottom. I glance over my shoulder and see Camden.

"What are you doing?"

"Relax and enjoy yourself." His hands skate up my rib cage and graze the underside of my breasts.

I jam my elbow into his stomach and muster all my strength to break free, but I'm sandwiched in between Trish and him. He becomes bolder and kneads my nipples.

"Let go!" I reach behind me and grab two fistfuls of his hair and yank forward.

"Goddamn it!" he yelps, relinquishing his grip on me.

I whirl on him. "How dare you?"

"Don't be such a prude," Trish says.

"He touched my breasts."

"Oh, for Christ's sake, it's just dancing," she chides, exasperated. "You're too uptight, honey. Chill and have a great time."

"Yeah. What's the big deal?" Camden asks.

"I'm leaving." I sprint into the horde of people and rush towards the exit.

"What is your problem?" Trish takes ahold of my arm.

"I don't like him."

"He seems cool."

"Stay and have fun. I'll catch an Uber home."

"Are you serious? The party is just getting started."

"Trish, I appreciate you inviting me, but I need to go."

Camden appears beside me, holding two red Solo cups. "I'm truly sorry for my despicable behavior, but I come bearing gifts." He offers the drinks to Trish and me.

"No, thank you," I say.

"You sure? It's nonalcoholic, just straight punch. Figured you didn't drink."

"Ah, come on. Cut him some slack, he apologized."

I notice everyone dancing is doing so provocatively. Maybe that's the norm, and I am being too tense. It wouldn't hurt to hang out for a while.

"Okay, but I'm leaving in thirty."

"I'll drink to that." Trish swallows a big gulp of her drink. "Let's finish shaking our groove things."

"I'm going to enjoy the scenery for a bit."

She shrugs. "Suit yourself."

The pair walk to the middle of the makeshift dance floor and resume their sexually explicit tango. I find an unoccupied corner of the sofa and squeeze in. I sip on the fruity concoction Camden gave to me. It's very sweet, but true to his word, it lacks alcohol. Twenty minutes or so later, my brain becomes foggy.

"Hey, are you okay?" Camden asks, stooping in front of me.

"I'm not feeling so hot," I slur. "I need to use the bathroom."

"There's a line for the one down here, but you can use the one upstairs to the left."

Overwhelming dizziness assails me as I rise to my feet.

"Do you want me to help you?"

"N-no." I stumble across the room and languidly climb the stairs. Luckily, I make it inside the bathroom unscathed.

I'm quickly losing control of my faculties and tumble to the vinyl tile. I'm disoriented and nauseated. Something isn't right. I gain enough composure to pull my cell phone from my purse, planning to call Dom, but it's like my mouth is stuffed with cotton. I won't be able to form one coherent syllable. I manage to click on the text message icon and select the Google Maps option to send my location along with a single word—*help*. Accomplishing this task was no easy feat. Contacting my father is a definite no, and I prefer not to involve Patrick. Though Dom's been distant lately, I have faith he'll come to my rescue.

Within seconds, I'm completely immobile, though I remain conscious. My cell phone rings a couple of times, but I'm incapable of answering it. The bathroom door opens to reveal Trish and Camden.

"We're going to have an incredible time together," Camden jeers, lifting me from the floor. "Grab her purse and cell."

He carries me into a bedroom and places me on the bed. I lie panic-stricken as he strips me.

"I knew your body would be stunning." He tugs my panties off and widens my legs. "Trish will have her fun first, then it'll be my turn to play."

"Don't fret, sweetie. By morning, you won't remember anything," Trish taunts. "Camden paid me a thousand bucks to lure you here."

"Trish and I are going to take special care of you. We've been doing this for a long time. She brings me the girls, and I pay her."

I will my paralyzed limbs into action, but to my horror they lie lifeless.

"Eat her pussy," Camden demands.

Garbled sounds escape my throat in protest. Trish crawls onto the bed and buries her face between my thighs. Camden uses his cell phone to record the interaction. The distorted scene unfolds in slow motion.

"So fucking hot," he groans. "Finger fuck her."

Tears prick my eyes as she savagely enters my center.

"On your knees." Camden frees his hardness before getting on the bed behind Trish and yanking her panties down. He slams into her as she continues violating me. All the while he records their detestable crime. I orgasm, my body betraying me. Another wave of dizziness hits me.

"This video will be a wonderful addition to the collection," he grunts.

My vision wanes by the second, drawing me closer to darkness.

"I'm coming!" he roars. "Shit, baby, that felt amazing."

"Her pussy is drenched," Trish drawls.

"Let me have a taste." His lips descend to hers, and they share a passionate kiss. "Damn, that's good."

"Put your cock in her mouth. I've tasted her, so it's only fair she returns the favor."

"Here." He gives her the phone. "Make sure you get a close-up."

He pries my jaw open and shoves his soft manhood into my lax mouth. "You're the perfect whore."

"Like that, uppity slut?" Trish mocks.

Inhaling air into my lungs becomes laborious, dangerously slowing my breathing.

He pulls his penis from my mouth. "Open her legs."

Trish moves above my head and spreads my incapacitated limbs for Camden's sexual assault. He positions his erection at my entrance and slowly pushes forward.

There's a loud bang. "Motherfucker!"

Dom.

Camden is thrown off the bed, and Trish screams. A fight ensues, and I black out.

Dom

Pepper still sleeps, though it's close to one o'clock in the afternoon. It's blind luck I was only thirty minutes from the address she texted. Drew and I were at a bar. We'd been drinking beer and shooting pool for several hours. It wasn't where I wanted to be on a Saturday night, but I was driving myself insane staring at my computer screen, watching her. *My obsession.* I needed something to occupy my mind. Drew readily agreed to accompany me, but Jensen declined to join us due to having a prior engagement with Sarah.

After reading her message, I hastily exited the establishment, shoving anyone in my path to the grimy floor. Drew chased behind me but refrained from asking questions until we were ensconced in the car. He knew from my demeanor the situation was grim and explanations could wait. Time was of the essence. My trepidation increased when my repeated calls were not answered. Once arriving at the gated community, I delivered an uppercut to the security guard, laying him flat because the bastard wouldn't let me through. We barged into the house and searched the first level in record speed before heading upstairs. I found her being sexually assaulted and snapped. If Drew wasn't there to pull me off Camden, I would've beaten him to a bloody pulp. The bitch didn't get a free pass for being a woman; she tasted my right hook. My revenge was short-lived because I needed to see to Pepper's health and safety, but I'm nowhere near done.

I arranged for a doctor to meet me at home instead of taking her to a hospital. Confidentiality is of the utmost importance. Police involvement would impede achieving my vengeance. No evidence of intercourse was found, to my relief. Her heart rate and blood pressure were low enough to cause concern but not life-threatening. A watchful eye was kept on her until both stabilized. The doctor said Pepper's symptoms coincide with the effects of Rohypnol and assured me she would be fine once the drug ran its course before he departed.

I kept an observant eye on Pepper while orchestrating my special brand of vigilante justice without having to bloody my hands. Granted, I preferred to deal with the perpetrators myself but didn't want to leave Pepper. For her own protection, I installed a GPS chip inside her cell phone. Now, I'll always know where she is. I gaze at her and tuck a wayward curl behind her ear. It's strange having Pepper lying next to me in my bed. This slip of a girl has implanted herself into the marrow of my bones, becoming an integral substance required for my survival. How the fuck did I allow that to happen? I value my self-control above all else—it's priceless—but she fucking obliterated it. And, goddamn, I want to cause her pain because of it. I've evaded emotional entanglements with women since Lauren, and I refuse to have my peace shattered now. That's the reason why I distanced myself from her. I needed to collect my thoughts and reevaluate the purpose of my pursuit. She's a means to an end, a summer fling. My goal is to corrupt and defile my sweet angel. Afterwards, I'll rip her wings off and set the motherfuckers on fire.

Finally, Pepper's eyelids flutter open and brown irises land on me. She rapidly blinks to focus her glazed orbs.

"Where am I?" she asks, dazed.

"My mansion."

"I'm naked."

"My housekeeper washed your clothes."

"Why? How did I get here?"

"You put yourself in danger last night," I bark, causing her to wince. I will myself to calm down. Pepper needs to be taught the error of her ways, but she has to recover first.

"What?"

"You were slipped a roofie."

"Roofie?" She props herself up on the pillows.

"It's a date rape drug."

"I was raped?" she asks, fear reflected in her voice.

"No, I arrived in time to stop it, and a doctor examined you, confirming you weren't raped."

"You saved me?"

"Yes."

She studies my face, my statement giving her pause. "How did you know where to find me?"

"You sent me a text."

"Trish and I were dancing." She rubs her temples. "Then nothing. My mind is drawing a blank. God, I have a terrible headache."

"Side effects of the drug. It'll pass." I grab the aspirin and bottled water on the nightstand. "Take these."

"Thank you." She pops both pills into her mouth and chugs down most of the cool drink.

"Camden Bailey and Allison Cox, aka Trish, set you up."

"That can't be true."

"You're so fucking naïve," I snap. "She's not an intern at my company."

"Trish works in marketing." Tears fill her eyes. "We had… we had lunch together."

"Camden snuck her into the building through the garage. You didn't see her before or after that day, correct?"

"No, but we met last week, and her mom had surgery—"

"All lies. She doesn't attend Duncan University either. The woman is a professional con artist with dozens of aliases and burner phones. She wore a wig and contacts so you wouldn't be able to accurately identify her."

"They wouldn't have gotten away with this."

"They're pros and have been doing this for years. They follow a very methodical process that includes bathing their victim after they're done. You would've woken up, sore between the legs, with no recollection of the events, the mysterious Trish gone and Camden pleading ignorance. Trust me, the DA wouldn't have pursued charges due to lack of evidence. They're predators, and they led you right to the fucking slaughter."

"How do you know all this?"

"They were interrogated."

"So, they've been arrested, then?"

"I made sure justice was served."

"How?" she asks, alarmed. "What did you do?"

"I employ different types of individuals. Some operate within the scope of the law and others do not. The fewer details you know, the better, but they'll never claim another victim again."

"Are they… are they dead?"

"No, but they should be. What if I did have them killed?"

"It's not your place to pass judgment."

"An eye for an eye, a tooth for a tooth."

"It's better to turn the other cheek."

"Good will never triumph over evil. One day you'll learn that."

She's silent for a moment. "Why me?"

"Camden has a penchant for virgins."

"The pot calling the kettle black," she spat.

"The only virgin I want is you."

"How does he know I'm a virgin? she asks accusingly.

"I found out about you because Camden has a big fucking mouth. You both attended the same school, and college campuses are breeding grounds for gossip."

"Who can I trust?"

"No one, least of all me."

"But you saved me."

"For my own selfish purposes."

"I don't believe you."

"No one takes my toy when I'm not done playing with it yet." I get out of the bed. "Your purse is on the dresser, and the bathroom is through that door. I'll have food brought to you." I leave the room.

I'm fucking restless. Goddamn, Pepper drives me crazy.

CHAPTER 17

Pepper

I check my cell phone, and, not surprisingly, I have dozens of missed calls and texts from my father and Patrick. I quickly type out a message.

Me: Sorry I missed church, but I had a bad case of food poisoning.

Dad: I stopped by the condo and you were not there!

Me: I went to the hospital.

Patrick: Feel better, sis.

Me: Thanks.

I hate lying, but the truth can't be known. Questions would be asked, and Dom could get into a heap of trouble. I can't betray him. Whatever he did was for me, though his methods are unsavory. I head to the bathroom and shower. Afterwards, I don a T-shirt and lounge pants belonging to Dom, since I couldn't find my own clothes, then leave the bedroom in search of him. Doors line both sides of the expansive hallway. How many rooms are there? Gold accents shimmer through the glossy marble floors. Surely this is a palace. I turn the corner and bump into a woman, causing her to drop the tray of food she's carrying.

"I'm so sorry." I help her gather the broken shards of glass.

"It's fine, dear."

My five-six frame towers over the short, thin woman. Her silver-gray hair is styled perfectly in a French twist. She's the epitome of professionalism.

"You must be the housekeeper."

"Yes, please call me Jackie, short for Jacqueline. And you're Pepper."

"I am. It's nice to meet you."

"Likewise, dear."

"I suppose you were bringing me this lovely meal." I sniff. "Butternut squash soup?"

"Yes, and there's plenty more in the kitchen."

"Great. I'm starving."

"Follow me. I'll clean this mess up later."

"I can do that, it's my fault."

"I won't hear of it. You're a guest."

"Are you sure?"

"Of course. Now come on so I can get you fed."

"All right."

We walk down the spiral staircase and step into the opulent foyer. Beautiful modern sculptures rest on pedestals, reminding me of the art museums I've visited in the past. My pace slows as I take in the lavish surroundings. Jackie is patient and doesn't rush me. A large family portrait sits over the fireplace in the living room; the typical all-American family. I wonder if his parents are still married. Envy stabs at me for being denied this. Life was never perfect for me, but my mom made it bearable, and then she was gone. Dom is no more than eight years old in the photo. Behind that big bright smile is a mischievous little boy. A single moment captured in time tells me more about Dom than he would ever willingly disclose to me. It's clear he had a happy childhood and wonderful support system. When did the glow in his twinkling eyes diminish, and how can I get it back? Maybe we're different sides of the same coin. The light in my eyes died the same day my mother did. Two traumatized people can't help each other— inevitably, we'd collide and implode. I'm staying the course knowing this.

We pass a glass wall, and beyond is an abundance of greenery, colorful flowers, and rustic furniture. The ceiling and walls enclosing the room are also glass. Situated in the center of the room is an enormous circular fish tank filled with a plethora of marine life.

"What is this called?"

"Solarium."

"It's so vibrant and breathtaking."

"I spend at least an hour in there a day, reading a book. It's my favorite room in the entire mansion."

"I'm so jealous."

"Stop by for a spell after you're done eating."

"Maybe."

That definitely will not be happening. I don't want to overstay my welcome. I'll eat, get dressed, then be on my way. I would've left already if it weren't for my gnawing belly. We continue on and step into a gorgeous dining room.

"Have a seat, and I'll be right back."

The rectangular table is positioned before a large window with a sparkling chandelier hanging above it. Twelve cream-colored upholstered chairs surround the polished wood. This room has a fireplace as well. The kitchen is connected by an open doorway, and I watch Jackie go about her task. Soon, she's placing a huge bowl of the fragrant soup in front me and a tall glass of tea.

She sits in the chair beside me. "Bon appétit."

"You're not eating?"

"I ate earlier."

"Oh, okay." I down a hearty spoonful. "This is really delicious."

"It's my grandmother's recipe."

I devour the tasty bisque in minutes.

"Would you like more?"

"No, I'm stuffed." I take a small sip of the too-sweet drink. "How long have you worked for Dom?"

"Three years."

"What sort of boss is he?" I could kick myself. Obviously, subtlety is not my forte, but I'm too curious about solving the Dominic Stone puzzle to pass up the opportunity to gather information.

"I couldn't ask for a kinder and more generous employer. My husband was diagnosed with prostate cancer. I missed a lot of work to take him to chemotherapy treatments, but Dominic still paid my salary and even a bonus for medical expenses."

"How is your husband now?"

"Great, and cancer-free."

"That's wonderful news."

She peers at me, knowingly. "You're intrigued by him."

I smile. "What gave it away?"

"A word of advice." Her tone turns serious. "Dominic is a good man, but a broken one. Tread cautiously."

Her warning chills me to the bone, but she means well. She's telling me what I already discerned. Dom is a very dark soul.

"Where is he?"

"I saw him heading towards the basketball court not long ago. Most likely, that's where he is."

"Can you take me to him?"

"Sure."

We walk in silence until we come to a set of double doors.

"I'll put your clothes on the bed for you."

"I appreciate everything."

"It was a pleasure. Perhaps we'll meet again."

"Perhaps."

She squeezes my shoulder, then ambles off. I inhale a reassuring breath before going inside. The sight of him impairs my cognitive abilities. Dom fluently dribbles the ball down the court. I'm not a sports girl, but he could make me change my mind. He's shirtless, providing me full access to watch the play of his sleek muscles bunch and flex. His shorts cling to his sweat-soaked body. He leaps into the air and slam dunks the ball into the basket. He spots me, and the predatory glint in his eyes sends me on alert. Should I stay or flee? At his approach, I involuntarily step back, survival instinct kicking in. He notices the small movement and smirks, amused by my fear of him. I will my resisting feet to remain motionless. He comes to a stop directly in front of me, so close I can see my reflection in his molten amber eyes. I'm enchanted. I've seen movies where vampires ensnared their unsuspecting victims, rendering them docile in order to drain their life force. But this is real life. Creatures of lore are found in fiction, or are they? Could Dom be one of the infamous undead?

My very own Count Dracula. Why else would I be so drawn to him?

Perspiration drips from his golden strands and lands on his mangled flesh. My entranced gaze follows a single trail of the salty liquid until it loses momentum and disappears at the corner of his captivating lips. I lift my hand, determined to run my fingers along his scars, but he brutally clasps my wrist.

He presses his nose to mine. "What the fuck are you doing?"

Undeterred, I lick Dom's damaged skin and his unique spicy flavor explodes on my tongue. A deep rumble tears from his mouth. He twists his large hand in my hair and jerks my head back.

"Do you know what happened to the chicken that tried to cross the road?" he whispers in my ear

"No."

"It got hit by a Mack truck. Careful, you're the chicken in this scenario. Go get dressed. We're leaving." He flings me backwards.

CHAPTER 18

Dom

I can't believe I'm bringing Pepper to my parents' house for dinner. She looked at me like I had a dick protruding from my forehead when I told her our destination. I see the reaction of each family member in my mind's eye. Jensen will glare disapprovingly while Drew laughs his ass off. Dad will give me a thumbs-up. Mom and Sarah will discuss the possibility of a winter-themed wedding and a spring baby shower. I maneuver my vehicle left into my childhood neighborhood. My brothers and I were well-known hell-raisers among the residents. Finding parking is always difficult, but I manage to find a spot a few houses down from my parents'.

"Are you sure this is okay?" Pepper asks, wringing her hands.

"Relax, it's fine."

"But I'm an outsider."

"Stop overthinking," I snap, getting out of the car.

Pepper's sexy high heels beat a rapid staccato on the pavement as she tries to match my long strides. We walk down the pathway and up the porch stairs. I hear boisterous laugher and revelry coming from inside. The small, quaint dwelling has pretty much remained the same. My parents are sentimental and very resistant to change. They did agree to have the kitchen expanded to add a sufficient dining space.

"I figured your parents would live in a big, fancy house."

"They refuse to relocate. There are a lot of fond memories for them here."

"Are there fond memories for you here too?"

"Yes," I answer, pushing open the front door.

Everyone's attention turns towards Pepper and me. The conversation stops, the blare of the television the only sound in the living room. My mother's hawklike gaze studies Pepper, and a wide smile spreads across her face. She rushes over from the sofa to give me a hug and kiss on the cheek.

"And who might you be?"

"My name is Pepper, ma'am." Pepper holds out her hand.

My mom embraces her instead. "Call me Edith."

"Okay, Edith it is."

"Are you Dominic's girlfriend, perhaps?" she asks, eyes lighting up.

"She's an intern at his company," Jensen answers. "Is it customary to invite a teenage employee to your parents' home for dinner?"

"She's not a teenager," I growl at the same time Pepper says, "I'm twenty."

"That makes you old enough to be her father," Jensen scolds.

Pepper fidgets in embarrassment.

"Quit being a jerk." Drew jabs Jensen in the arm.

"Honey, don't be a sourpuss," Sarah chides.

If my nieces and nephew weren't here, I'd throttle their father. My mother escorts Pepper around the living room to finish introductions. Technically, Pepper and my brothers have met, kind of, but no one needs to know the circumstances of that unfortunate mishap.

"Hi, Uncle Dom," Clara, my oldest niece, greets. "Long time, no see."

I give her a one-arm hug and kiss on the forehead. "Sorry I've been MIA, kid"

"Hey, quit calling me kid. I'm practically an adult."

"You're fourteen." I chuckle.

"Fifteen in three months," she says indignantly.

"You're right. Forgive my faux pas," I placate her.

"Apology accepted." She peers at me with sad sky-blue eyes. "I miss you, a lot."

I love all my brother's children, but Clara and I have a special bond. I was at the hospital during her birth. Once Jensen placed her in my arms, I was completely ensnared. While Clara spent most weekends with me, the other girls preferred to stay home. Then I became a bitter prick, not fit to be in the company of my impressionable young niece.

"I know I've been a shitty uncle, but I'll make it up to you, I promise."

"Shitty doesn't begin to cover it."

"Hey, watch your mouth, young lady," Sarah says, then points at me. "And you, stop being a bad influence."

"Is the food done, woman?" my father asks my mother jokingly. "I'm starving."

"Oh, you big oaf. One of these days I'm going to make you fend for yourself," she huffs and stomps to the kitchen.

Pepper sits next to Sarah, and the two strike up a conversation.

Jensen approaches me. "Darling, I need to have a private word with your uncle."

"Keep your promise," Clara says to me, then saunters off.

I lean against the wall. "Not now."

"You've lost your mind."

"You're wasting your time."

"Clara will be Pepper's age in six years. What would you do if she brought a man eighteen years her senior home?"

"I'd kill him."

"You're a fucking hypocrite."

"I accept who I am."

"That's your problem, you think rules don't apply to you."

"Dinner's ready," our mother announces.

We all trail into the dining area, but Jensen steps in my way. "There has to be a minuscule amount of human decency left in you. Leave the poor girl alone."

"A predator never releases its prey."

Pepper

Dom settles into the chair next to me. His father says a quick prayer and then we dig in. The family's lighthearted banter is contagious. I'm not excluded, and everyone is very welcoming, except for Jensen. He really hates me. His constant glare is unnerving. I try my best to ignore him and focus on the delicious lamb chop, roasted red skin potatoes, kale, and buttered roll on my plate.

"Everything tastes really amazing, Edith. It's rare I have a home-cooked meal."

"Thank you so much," she says, glowing.

"Mom's cooking is barely edible." Drew winks at me. "No need to suck up."

Peals of laughter erupt around the table. Drew looks vaguely familiar, but I can't put my finger on it. I hadn't noticed before because I was spread wide on top of Dom's desk.

"You wicked boy." She whacks him on the head with a wooden spoon.

"Ouch, just joking."

Dom even participates in the family-friendly squabble. This is a side of him I've never seen. He's almost… almost normal.

The love between them is tangible. What draws my attention most is Howard, the patriarch of the Stone clan. My father and he are polar opposites. He's all cheer, fun, and jokes. There's a hole in my heart only the love of a father can fill. Russell Bryant has never shown me an ounce of affection. A horrible event must've happened in his life that made him so hateful.

"Who wants peach cobbler and vanilla ice cream?" Edith asks.

A collective chorus of "me" echoes throughout the room.

I'm served a large portion of dessert that leaves me stuffed. I'll need to exercise for forty hours straight to work off the calories I consumed.

"All right, skedaddle, so I can clean up," Edith says, gathering plates and silverware.

"I'll take care of this for you and wash the dishes too," I offer.

"Bless your heart." She smiles. "That isn't necessary."

"I insist. It's the least I can do."

"You are such a sweetheart."

"I'll help you," Drew says.

"Thanks," I say.

The group retreats to the living room while Drew and I clear the table.

He seems so familiar. Where do I know him from? I intently study his face, then suddenly two and two click together.

"You're D. Soul."

I recall watching his performance on one of those award shows.

He bows. "At your service."

"My roommate loves your song, umm… shoot, I can't think of the name."

"'Missing Pieces.'"

"Yes, that's the one."

"I'm taking a hiatus for the interim, but you and your roommate are invited to my next gig."

"Wow, thanks."

"No prob."

I wash the dishes, then hand them to Drew to dry.

"How are you?" he asks, concern in his eyes.

I regard him strangely. "I'm fine. Why did—" Then it dawns on me. "Dom told you about last night?"

I can't believe Dom would betray me by discussing the humiliating incident.

"I was there."

We face each other, our chore forgotten.

"You must think I'm a moron for putting myself in that situation."

"No, definitely not. You were taken advantage of."

"If Dom hadn't come…"

"He would never let anything happen to you."

"Your brother is confusing."

"He cares for you a great deal."

"How do you know?" I ask, daring to hope.

"He's been different since meeting you."

"Different?"

"More volatile, short-tempered, and violent."

My elation dissipates with each adjective spoken.

"He's afraid. Please don't ever tell him I said that." Drew chuckles. "He'd rather rip out his own toenails than admit weakness."

"I bring out the worst in him," I say dejectedly.

"You do, but you're also good for him."

"What you're saying doesn't make any sense."

"A hurricane is the most violent storm on earth. An eye forms in the center as the storm system rotates faster and faster. The eye is calm and clear."

"Why are you telling me this?" I ask, confused.

"Metaphorically speaking, Dom is a hurricane. Find his center and bring him peace."

"That's bullshit, Drew, and you know it," Jensen says in anger.

I didn't hear him come into the kitchen.

"You have a stick so far up your ass, it's coming through your goddamn mouth," Drew says in annoyance.

"You're weaving a fucking fairy tale," Jensen snarls.

"What do you have against me?"

"It's not personal."

"Could've fooled me," I say sarcastically.

"You're infatuated, I get it, but he needs a woman he can have a meaningful relationship with."

"Dom is an adult. He doesn't need you to make decisions for him." I refuse to back down.

"I'll give you twenty thousand dollars to disappear."

"Excuse me?" I ask indignantly, angered by his gall to proposition me.

"Dom is going to murder you, man," Drew says in disbelief.

"Fucking asshole," Dom growls, charging Jensen and landing a blow to his solar plexus.

He immediately retaliates, punching Dom in the face. I stand there, terrified, watching the vicious exchange.

Drew wedges himself between them. "Stop it, stop it," he whispers. "Your kids are in the next room, and Dom, don't break Mom's heart."

"We're going to finish this," Dom vows, wiping the blood from his lip.

"Thinking with your cock will land you in hot water."

"Dom, please stop," I plead. "I don't want you and Jensen fighting because of me."

"It's time for us to go."

We say our goodbyes, to the disappointment of Dom's mother, but I promised to come to another family dinner sooner rather than later. Unfortunately, it's probably a promise I can't keep.

Pepper

Dom's sour attitude was palpable in the small confines of his car during the entire drive. My attempts to engage in chitchat were met with seething silence. His mood remains firmly in place as he follows me inside my condo. I'm relieved to finally slip out of my high heels. I trudge to the couch on sore feet and plunk down. Dom paces back and forth in agitation.

"You would've accepted his bribe if I hadn't intervened," he accuses, turning wild eyes on me.

"How can you say that?" I ask, standing. "Money doesn't mean anything to me."

"You're a lying bitch!" he shouts.

"See yourself out," I snap, stomping towards my bedroom.

He grabs the nape of my neck and slams me into the wall, creating a crack in the plaster. "Turn your back on me again, and I'll slit your fucking throat."

I'm dazed by the painful impact. "Dom, please—
"

He clasps the lower half of my face, squeezing so brutally, I'm afraid my jawbone will be crushed. "Shh… it's time for you to meet the beast."

Dom transforms, morphing into the savage he warned me about. The change isn't physical, making it imperceptible to the naked eye. It's in the menacing aura he emits, as if his DNA has suddenly altered, losing the element that defines his humanity and turning into something alien. The unseen force shifts the air, suffocating me, and raises the fine hairs covering my body. He pinches my nipple, tearing an agonized scream from my throat.

"To reach ultimate bliss, one must experience pain and pleasure simultaneously."

He releases my jaw and shoves his fingers beneath the waistband of my panties, ruthlessly attacking my clit.

"Feeling the push and pull of both is conflicting but also the sweetest ecstasy."

"Dom," I moan, widening my stance to allow him better access.

"Eager for another journey to Hell, I see."

"I am. Please take me there," I beg, no reservations about my choice to stray further into the bowels of damnation. Though I know each visit will lead me deeper into the abyss until I'm trapped, I'm unable to find my way to the light.

His warm, tantalizing tongue drifts along the column of my neck while the relentless onslaught on my most sensitive nerve endings draws me closer to gratification. For him, I abandon the lessons beaten into me as a child. For him, I risk the ire of God and my father. I slump forward and dig my sharp fingernails into his hard biceps, no longer capable of supporting my own weight.

"The scent of your arousal is driving me in-fucking-sane," Dom mutters, briskly rubbing my engorged nub.

My vulva swells, heating my core and making me wetter. Then I plateau, attaining orgasmic release through a series of rhythmic contractions. I bite his shoulder, riding the wave of euphoria until the tide ebbs and I'm left panting.

"Your reprieve is over," he growls.

The fantasy I've longed for is within my grasp, but suddenly fear overwhelms me. If I give in, my descent from grace will truly be complete. "I'm not ready."

"Ready or not, here I come," Dom murmurs, seizing my hair and dragging me into my bedroom.

He throws me onto the bed and undresses while his riveting gaze focuses on me. I swiftly vault to my hands and knees, but instead of using my temporary freedom to escape, I ogle him, transfixed. Dom's sculpted figure rivals the Roman gladiators of the past. His imposing girth and length heighten my apprehension. Surely, he'll sever me in two. I scurry to the other side of the bed at his approach. He leisurely strolls to the door, shutting and locking it before facing me again. The accelerated rise and fall of his athletic chest belies his tranquil façade.

"You knew this day was coming."

"But now it's here, and I'm scared."

"There's only one way to conquer your fears."

"Protection! We can't have sex without a condom. I could get pregnant."

"I had a vasectomy."

"Listen, let's—" Dom pounces before I can finish my plea, catching me off guard. I'm tussled to the bed, and a scuffle ensues. My clothing is briskly torn from me, and my wrists are pinned above my head using one hand. He effortlessly wrestles my thighs apart and positions his manhood at my opening.

"Please… Dom… don't."

He viciously drives forward, ripping a gut-wrenching wail from the pit of my stomach.

"Relax, I'm almost done," he says gruffly.

"There's more?" I ask incredulously.

"Yes."

"No! I can't take any more." Tears spill from my eyes. "It hurts so much."

Dom ignores my sobs and tunnels through my tight sheath, commencing his violent intrusion. He hikes my left leg over his shoulder, spreading me wider for his marauding penis. One more crude lunge ruptures my hymen, inflicting unimaginable agony. My narrow channel is stretched, surpassing its limits.

He licks my tears. "So, that's what a fallen angel's tears taste like… sorrow and regret. Delicious."

He propels his hips between my thighs. My slick heat combined with my virgin blood eases his invasion and lessens the ache of his feral claiming. Each thrust kindles the embers within me to a scorching firestorm, enhancing my pleasure. He pulls free of my body, then smears his bloody hardness across my quavering lips. It's atrocious, beyond abominable, but I yearn for more of his addictive wickedness. Dom buries his erection to the hilt inside my welcoming warmth once again as his tongue sweeps into my mouth, sealing our ill-fated joining with a blood oath. I continuously pondered what my first kiss would be like. The actual reality surpasses my wildest dreams. I plant my feet flat on the mattress and surge upwards to meet his plundering breadth. We cling to each other, gripped by our untamed passion. Dom's vigorous strokes tow me further under the spell of his intoxicating lunacy, but in the midst of the chaos, there's serenity.

"Only in Hell can madness bring peace," I whisper against his lips.

"Hell is a fucking paradise with many hidden treasures. I'll introduce you to them all."

I spontaneously combust, igniting in a fiery haze. The conflagration is so powerful, it blinds me.

"Oh my God," I scream, my depths clamping down on his pillaging shaft.

Dom pumps into me in a frenzy, releasing an ear-splitting roar as he comes.

We bore into each other's eyes, stunned at the ferocity of our union. "Is it always like this?"

"No," he answers curtly and rolls onto his back.

I'm bereft. He doesn't hold me; there's no admission of undying love. He erects an invisible wall, separating us. We might as well be strangers. This is all wrong. I should be bathing in the afterglow of our phenomenal lovemaking, but Dom turned something beautiful, ugly. His parents are the embodiment of happily ever after. How can he not believe in it?

"You said unconditional love doesn't exist between a man and woman."

"It doesn't."

"Your parents have been married for several decades, so obviously their love isn't conditional."

"They're the exception to the rule."

"And Jensen and Sarah? Based on their interactions at dinner, I'd say they're madly in love. It seems there's more than one exception to the rule."

He regards me knowingly. "I warned you not to fancy yourself falling in love with me."

"It's too late."

"What you're feeling is lust, infatuation even, but it definitely isn't love."

"I'm not as dumb as you think I am."

"Obviously you are." He roughly flips me onto my stomach and enters my inflamed center in one fluid motion. "This is the only thing I'll give to you."

"Be gentle," I whimper, clutching the sweat-soaked sheets.

"That," Dom kisses my ear, "I can't do."

He delivers bone-jarring strokes to my already ravaged passage, thus my unorthodox initiation to sex continues into the wee hours of the morning.

CHAPTER 20

Pepper

I gradually come to awareness. My entire body is riddled with pain, particularly my nether region. Dried blood and semen stain my inner thighs as well as the bedding, evidence of last night's erotic delights. The distinctive aromatic scent of sex permeates the air. I'm alone in the bed, the spot beside me cool to the touch.

"Dom?" I call but receive no answer. Perhaps he went home after I fell asleep. He could've been courteous and left a note. It's silly, but I wanted to wake up next to him. Maybe I am the stupid girl he accuses me of being.

My aching muscles protest as I sit upright. I check the time on my cell phone.

8:17

Oh no! I'm seventeen minutes late for work. I dial Lloyd and quickly rattle off an apologetic voice message when he doesn't pick up. Sleeping through three alarms attests to the strenuous mating that ended only mere hours before. I hop out of bed but tumble to the floor. My lower back and legs throb. It's like someone took a battering ram to me. My eyes land on the cross hanging above my bed. It beats down on me, harsher than the rays of the sun on a hot day in July. I clasp my hands together, intending to pray and beg for forgiveness, but words escape me. I can't do it, because I'm not sorry. I enjoyed every second of Dom's barbaric coupling. What's the point of atoning when I'd do it again in a heartbeat? I clamber to unsteady feet and hobble to the bathroom.

I arrive to my cubicle at ten o'clock on the dot. I power on my computer and set to respond to emails. The first is regarding visits from family and friends. Both are no longer welcomed at Stone Incorporated. Everyone must don an employee or visitor's badge while inside the building, no exceptions. The new policy will be fully enforced by security. No doubt this came about due to Camden and Allison's treachery. The second is from Dom, instructing me to come to his office. Lloyd rushes by but backtracks after spotting me.

"I've been searching for you all morning," he admonishes.

"I'm so sorry for being late. I called, but you didn't answer, so I left a voice message."

"I haven't had time to check messages," he says, flustered. "The office is in an uproar."

"What happened?"

"Come with me."

I notice the whispered conversations and flurry of activity that previously escaped my attention as we enter an empty conference room.

"Camden Bailey was found nearly beaten to death over the weekend. He's in critical but stable condition at Brentwood Hospital."

"Oh my God." Bile churns in my stomach.

"Two detectives are here questioning his direct coworkers and anyone who knew him from Duncan University, so they need to talk to you."

"He's stable, so he'll make a full recovery, right?"

"I'm not sure. The particulars of his injuries were not disclosed to me."

If he dies, I'll be an accomplice to murder.

"Did you know him well?"

"Just in passing."

"The detectives should be ready for you this afternoon."

"Okay," I croak.

"Don't worry. They're going to catch the psychopaths responsible." He squeezes my shoulders in reassurance before exiting the room.

God, please let him live.

Dom

My focus is on the chocolate goddess several floors below me, instead of the multimillion-dollar contract my lawyer sent for approval. A man of honor would've shown more care with an untried woman, but I fucked her ruthlessly. Pepper's pleas for mercy were ignored. I couldn't stop. The truth is, I didn't want to. I reveled in causing her pain, and seeing her virgin blood was the catalyst that fueled my cruelty to irredeemable heights. There's no remorse, not a pang of guilt. My only regret is not fucking her twice as hard.

Pepper marches into my office. She raises her chin in false bravado, which greatly amuses me. My predatory gaze roams over her body. Fuck, I love seeing her in pants. The fabric outlines her luscious curves splendidly. I adjust my hardening length.

"What am I going to say to the detectives?"

"You bled a lot." I pointedly stare between her legs. "How are you feeling?"

"I-I'm f-fine," she stutters.

"Good. Tell the detectives you were home Saturday night. All evidence linking you to Camden and Allison was destroyed. The security guard was paid off, and the list he had is gone. Surveillance cameras in the neighborhood, wiped clean. No rock was left unturned. You're safe."

"There are dozens of witnesses who saw me with them at the party."

"Most of them were either drunk or high, probably both, and it was dark inside the house."

"What if Camden and Allison talk?"

"He recorded every sexual assault they ever committed, and those videos are now in my possession. Trust me, they'll keep quiet."

"Is there one of me?"

"Not anymore."

"Thank you for deleting it."

"You're welcome."

"They'll recover, right?"

"Camden will spend the remainder of his life wheelchair bound, and Allison's face resembles mine."

"I'm grateful you came to my rescue, but this is wrong."

"They deserve far worse." I walk around the desk to be closer to her.

"The Bible teaches—"

"Such a hypocrite." I finger the cross pendant lying above her ample breasts before snatching the necklace from around her neck. "You think wearing this absolves your sins?" I toss it into the garbage can.

"No!" she yells in outrage and tries to retrieve the mangled jewelry, but I slam her onto the desk.

"You need a reminder that your body is no longer a temple. It's mine to fuck… mine to abuse… mine to fill with cum."

"Let me go!" She vehemently struggles to stand.

"Stay still," I demand, grinding my elbow into her back.

I free my dick and yank her bottoms down. Splotches of bright red cover the pad attached to her panties.

"I'm hurt!" she cries. "Please, don't!"

I ram my throbbing erection inside her compact cunt, stretching her beyond capacity. I place my hand over her mouth to smother her piercing screams. The depravity in me comes to a boiling point, and her body will pay the price. I pound into her, unrestrained, hard and fast, putting all my strength behind each thrust. Pepper's muscles give in, yielding to accommodate my savagery. Her wet, hot cunt clenches, encasing my cock in an ironclad vise.

"Fuck!" I shout, pumping my hips at breakneck speed until I'm wrung dry.

My softening cock slips out of Pepper's snug pussy. A mixture of semen and blood spills from her center. I instantly harden to full mast, mesmerized by the sight.

She slides to the floor, sobbing. "I can't walk."

I carry her to my private apartment and fuck her again.

CHAPTER 21

Pepper

Immediately after arriving home, I discarded my clothes and ran a bubble bath. Sighing delightedly, I settle into the bathtub. Steam rises from the blazing water, creating my own personal sauna. I place a damp washcloth over my eyes. It's been a very trying day, and the hot bath relieves my stressed tendons. Contending with Dom and the detectives mentally drained me. I was directed to a vacant office and interrogated for an hour. The same questions were asked repeatedly, but I remained steadfast in my responses. I kept my nervousness at bay, or else suspicion would have fallen on me and possibly led to the prosecution of Dom. I'm confident we're in the clear.

I massage between my legs, smoothing my swollen folds. This morning I bled profusely. I panicked, thinking Dom caused serious damage, but a quick Google search alleviated my concerns.

166

Bleeding for a day or two after having sex for the first time is quite common. Soft music playing from my cell phone lying on top of the toilet is interrupted by the blaring ringtone. I hope it's not my father, or worse, Lester, calling. Groaning, I reluctantly sit up to see who it is. Mia's name flashes across the screen. Dang, I forgot to return her call. I click the speaker icon and lean back against the porcelain.

"Hello."

"Where have you been, Ms. Thing?" she asks good-naturedly.

"I had an eventful weekend," I reply vaguely.

That's an understatement.

"Partied too hard, huh?"

The decision was difficult, but I decide not to confide in Mia about Saturday night. I'm compelled to protect Dom, though I hate what he's done. The fewer people privy to the shady specifics, the better.

"Not really. I only stayed for a little while, then went home."

I feel dreadful for lying to her.

"Boring! Is that your definition of eventful?"

"No, actually. Dom and I had sex."

"Eek!" she exclaims.

"Please have some sympathy for my poor eardrums."

"Give me the deets."

"He's profound, violent, dominant… an unconventional lover."

"Sounds extreme."

"It was, and scary too."

"My God." Mia inhales a sharp breath. "Did he force you?"

"Yes and no."

"Umm... can you provide a bit more clarification?"

"Dom is a formidable man. I got scared and begged him to stop, but he wouldn't. He took what he wanted."

"He's a despicable pig!" she rages. "You need to go to the police!"

"I can't."

"Why not?"

"Don't judge me, okay? I liked it. He terrifies the crap out of me, but being with him is a rush."

"Whoa."

"Am I weird?"

"Fuck yeah. You're into that rough, kinky shit."

"Oh, hush, Mia."

"You're such a freak." She chortles.

"I shouldn't have told you," I grumble.

"Hey, I'm not knocking you. Some bitches need their ass beat to come." She cackles louder.

"My father is right about me," I say, resigned.

"Sugar plum, I'm yanking your chain. You're talking to a girl who threw up in a guy's mouth during a foursome. Who am I to judge anyone?"

I chuckle. "Oh, how could I forget? You called me at one in the morning, begging me to come get your sorry butt."

"You took care of me and cleaned up my chunky, smelly vomit."

"Please don't remind me of that rancid disgusting odor." I gag. "That's a memory I want wiped from my mind."

"Fun times." She laughs.

"I have some exciting news."

"Well, don't keep me in suspense, tell me."

"I'm tired." I yawn loudly. "We'll talk more tomorrow."

"Pepper Bryant, I will book a flight to California."

"If you insist."

"I do."

"D. Soul, aka Drew Stone, is Dom's brother."

"Oh. My. God!" she screeches.

"He invited us to his next show."

"I'm going to faint."

We talk and joke a while longer and then I finish my bath and go to bed.

Dom

For the last five minutes, I've stood at the foot of Pepper's bed as she slumbers, palming my stiff erection. Thoughts of her plagued me, preventing me from sleep, so here I am. I'd allow her traumatized

169

body a recovery period if I had an ounce of human decency. Sadly, for Pepper, I never acquired that particular characteristic. I undress, then climb onto the bed. Ever so gently, I pull her panties off and spread her legs, careful not to stir her too soon. I position my dick at her moist opening and drive home, sinking into her liquid heat.

She awakes, unleashing a deafening scream. The anguished sound feeds my sadistic soul and spurs me on. I roll my hips in a circular motion, pummeling in and out of her snug cunt.

"Dom, not so rough," she weeps, pushing my shoulders.

I lie flush atop her and secure her wrists against the bed, burrowing through her sopping wet passage. Heaven and Hell collide, fusing together, amplifying the ferociousness of our union. It's primal, unstable… liable to incinerate us both. Nothing else exists but this earth-shattering moment. The gravity of it isn't lost on me. Our bodies and minds merge. Fucking Pepper is becoming about something greater than sexual gratification. No woman has ever made me lose my shit the way she does. We share an impassioned kiss as our tongues intertwine in a sensual dance. I ram into her balls deep and grind against her pelvic bone, nudging her cervix. I swallow her moans of rapture as her spasming muscles milk my dick.

"Pepper," I groan, emptying my cum inside her scorching pussy.

I grasp her waist and flip to my back so she straddles me. My semi-hard dick grows to full mast again.

"Put your feet flat on the bed." Pepper does as she's told. "Now bounce up and down on my cock."

She proceeds tentatively, unsure of herself.

"No, that won't do. I know your secrets, your desires, your fantasies. Drop your fucking inhibitions and take my dick like the slut you aspire to be."

Pepper throws her head back and rides my shaft in abandon, liberating her inner slut. She'd rival the most seasoned adult film star. I click on the lamp for a better view and *fuck me.* Sweat illuminates her beautiful, dark complexion. I fixate on her pretty labia as it expands over my length and then my gaze roams upwards to watch the hypnotic jiggle of her heavy titties. She's a goddamn Siren. I sit up to feast on her nipples. She wraps her legs around me, crossing her ankles at the base of my spine. We move in sync, climaxing together in a maelstrom of explosions. Then we fall asleep in each other's embrace.

CHAPTER 22

Pepper

I'm incredibly happy this morning. Waking cocooned in Dom's strong embrace uplifted my spirits drastically. I assumed he'd be gone before sunrise. He kissed me goodbye and left to get ready for work. Perhaps he's turning over a new leaf, or maybe I'm reading too much into this small gesture. The hour of our clandestine rendezvous fast approaches. I finish up my work, then switch my computer to sleep mode.

"Hey, wanna join me for lunch?" Anthony asks, leaning over the side of my cubicle.

He's one of the dozen or so lead software engineers and is very friendly and graciously answers all my questions. I've learned a lot from him.

"Oh, umm—"

"Your ideas for program coding are amazing, and I'm hoping to bounce some ideas off you."

"Thank you," I say, my face heating at his praise.

"So, what do you say?"

Dom is waiting for me, but he shouldn't mind if I skip out this one time. Anyway, I'll see him later.

"Give me a sec."

"Great." He smiles, displaying cute dimples.

I text Dom, letting him know not to expect me.

"Let's go," I say, grabbing my purse.

"It's two-dollar taco Tuesday at the Mexican spot on the corner."

"Yum, my fave."

We chat amicably during the ten-minute walk. Anthony is a handsome guy and exudes masculine sex appeal. Totally Mia's type. He resembles Michael B. Jordan and looks to be in his mid-twenties. I could play Cupid and set up a blind date. I'll definitely keep that in mind. We enter the restaurant and are shown to a booth promptly. Shortly thereafter, a waitress stops by and takes our order.

"I'll be back," I say.

"All right."

I use the ladies' room, then head back to the dining area. A big smile graces my face, recalling last night. I stop, dumbfounded, finding Dom in the place of Anthony.

"What are you doing here? Where's Anthony?"

"Sit the fuck down." His thunderous countenance sends a jolt of uneasiness through me.

I slide into the booth.

"Was your smile for him?"

"No, it's not what—"

He bangs his fist on the table, startling me. "Don't fucking lie to me."

Just then the waitress brings the food. "Where's the other gentleman?"

Neither of us responds.

"Okay, well, enjoy." She hurries from the table.

"People will talk." Anthony is probably at the office telling everyone how Dom followed us here and demanded he leave. Only one conclusion can be drawn from his behavior.

"Let them."

"How did you know I'd be here?"

"At noon, you come to me. No questions and no exceptions. Disobey and I'll fuck you up."

"I'm not your property," I snap, not considering the consequences of my words.

"Go to the restroom and wait for me."

I shake my head, refusing to accept his treatment of me. He's being absurd and ruined one of the happiest days I've had in a while.

He stands, yanks me from the table, and drags me into the women's restroom. More than a few diners observe the exchange.

"You can't be in here."

He jerks me in front of the mirror. "Put your hands on the sink and keep them there."

"We could get caught at any moment," I say, doing as demanded.

Dom lifts my skirt and pull my panties to my knees.

"Not here, please."

"Your pussy belongs to me," he snarls. "It curves to my dick, welcoming Daddy home."

I bite my bottom lip and close my eyes, overpowered by the intense emotions Dom stirs in me. This man tantalizes all five of my senses to soaring heights.

"Look at me!" Dom shouts.

His eyes bore into mine through the mirror while he leisurely kisses along my neck. Dom hates his reflection, but he's too entranced to realize what he's doing. He penetrates me in a devastatingly slow stroke, reducing me to putty. Once his length is fully seated in my depths, he pauses briefly before withdrawing until only the mushroom-shaped tip remains, then starts the torture all over again.

"I want this every fucking day," he murmurs, moving his fingers between my thighs to strum and pluck my slippery clit.

My legs shake, weakened by his talented skills. He cups my chin, angling my head to feed me his tongue.

"Oh my God," I hear a woman shriek.

Dom and I are too immersed in passionate bliss to react. The conflagration in my center rapidly gains momentum, then bursts into a ball of orgasmic ecstasy. His thrusts become frenzied and uncoordinated.

"I fucking own you," he grunts, spilling his seed inside my body.

"Leave the premises immediately or I'm calling the police," a man says, scandalized.

The woman must've gone for the manager after catching us. Dom pulls himself out of me and stuffs his softening erection into his pants. He helps me make myself decent and then we exit the restroom hand in hand while the man stares daggers at us.

"Is everything good?" Patrick asks from beside me. "You don't seem yourself."

That's a loaded question. So much has happened since the start of summer, I'm getting whiplash. But today—I groan inwardly—was the straw that broke the camel's back. By the time I got back to the office, the gossip mill was teeming. The whispers and glares were awful. Even Lloyd gave me the cold shoulder. I spent the afternoon hiding in my cubicle. Dom and I need to have a serious conversation. His jealous behavior put my reputation on the line.

The deafening applause interrupts my thoughts. This week is the semi-annual revival at church. The pews are filled with members of the congregation.

I'd prefer to be home, but my father is becoming suspicious since I missed service on Sunday and yesterday. The guest speaker stands behind the pulpit, preaching the word of God. Her loud voice grates on my nerves.

I can't wait to visit Mia. Ice cream and in-person girl talk is desperately needed.

I glance at Lisa, who's a few rows ahead of me to the left. She was four, and I was nearly nine, when my father relocated us to California. The similarities between us are uncanny. It escaped my notice for all these years. We have the same build and facial features. Has no one ever suspected the truth?

"I'm fine," I answer. "I'm going to talk to Lisa after service."

"Bad idea."

"She's our sister."

"You can't tell her that."

"My lips are sealed. I just want to spend some time with her."

"Fine. Remember to keep quiet."

Once service concludes, I hug and kiss Patrick goodbye before seeking Lisa out. I spot her at the rear of the church leaning against the wall, eyes glued to her cell phone.

"Hi," I say.

She looks up. "Hey, how's it going?"

"I started an internship, so I've been busy. Having a good summer?"

"Yeah, just working and chillaxing with friends," Lisa answers.

"Super. Umm… well maybe we can hang out sometime."

"That would be great," she says excitedly. "How about next Saturday?"

"Sure, I'm available."

"Cool."

"Pepper, come here, please," my father says.

"See you then," I say.

"Looking forward to it."

I make my way over to him. "Yes?"

"Go to my office. I'll be up in a moment."

"Okay."

I go upstairs to his office and find Lester there. What does Dad have up his sleeve?

"I suppose my father asked you here too," I say, settling in the chair beside him.

"He did."

"Is something wrong?"

"We'll discuss it when your father gets here."

This can't be good.

"You two make a lovely couple," my father announces as he enters the room and sits behind his desk.

"We're not together."

Dad scowls at me disapprovingly. "That'll change very soon."

"What's this about?" The sooner this conversation is over with, the better.

"Lester tells me you're disinterested and aloof towards him."

"I didn't mean to seem that way."

"Lester is a good Christian man, and you're lucky to have his attention."

Once Mia and I move in together, this charade ends. I'll finally be free of both men. Right now, I have to bite my tongue.

"Lester, please accept my apology."

"All I ask is that you give us a real chance." He squeezes my hand. "I'm falling in love with you."

It's worse than I imagined. "This is moving too fast for me."

"We can take it slow."

"Thank you." I slide my hand out of his grasp. "I really should get going. It's late. Good night."

"Pray. God will guide you," Dad says.

I nod and rush from the room.

CHAPTER 23

Dom

"How did I get sucked into refereeing a fight between you two?" Drew asks, sulking. "I should be spending my Saturday afternoon in the company of a beautiful woman."

Jensen, Drew, and I climb into the boxing ring located in my home gym. The day of reckoning is here. No rules, headgear, mouth guard, or boxing gloves—just Jensen and me, bare-knuckle.

"This is long overdue," I say.

"Usually, adults solve their differences by having a civilized conversation," Drew deadpans.

"I'd rather beat Jensen black and blue."

"You talk a lot of shit, little brother. Perhaps you forgot I laid your ass out last time."

"I'm not an eighteen-year-old kid anymore."

"No, you're a thirty-eight-year-old degenerate."

"Dude, that's harsh," Drew says.

"She would've taken my offer if you hadn't interrupted us."

"Enough talking," I shout.

We square up against each other.

"Ahh, hell." Drew sighs and hastens to the corner of the ring.

"You need to be knocked down a peg or two," Jensen snarls.

"After this ass whooping, stop meddling in my fucking life."

I position my legs shoulder-width apart and place my left foot a half step ahead of the right. Jensen holds his right fist beside his chin and tucks his elbow against his rib cage while holding the left in front his face. I strike quick, jabbing him in the nose.

"Fuck!" Jensen bellows, blood spewing from his nostrils.

"You've lost your edge, big brother," I taunt.

He throws a punch, but I rotate my body, avoiding a blow to the head. I counterattack with a right hook, but Jensen parries, successfully evading the hit. Our skills are indicative of the lessons taught to us by our father as children.

"My edge is as sharp—"

I deliver an uppercut, and he crashes to the canvas. "What were you saying?"

"Goddamn, I felt that," Drew says.

"Shut the hell up," Jensen growls.

He swiftly hops to his feet and attacks, scoring a jab-cross combo to my face. From there, the brawl escalates. Blood and fists fly. I manage to maneuver Jensen against the ropes and batter his torso. A powerful blow is landed to my diaphragm, knocking the wind out of me and allowing Jensen to gain the upper hand. He tackles me to the canvas and straddles me.

"Guys, enough." Drew tries to separate us.

I block Jensen's descending fist and retaliate but miss my target, socking Drew in the groin instead.

He hunches over, clutching his cock and releasing a bloodcurdling roar. "Sweet baby Jesus! My chances of fatherhood are ruined!"

Jensen and I erupt into laughter.

"You assholes think this is funny?" He staggers out of the ring. "I'm telling Mom."

"There's ice in the freezer," I say.

"Fuck off."

Jensen moves to a sitting position. "I'm getting too old for this shit."

I push up on my elbows. "No more interfering in my business."

"Fine."

I nod towards his bloody face. "Sarah's going to have your ass."

"Tell me about it."

"If you'll excuse me." I stand. "I have somewhere important to be."

"Yeah, right," he scoffs. "You're going to see Pepper."

"Remember to stay in your lane, Jensen," I warn, stumbling from the ring.

Pepper

I pop the last orange slice in my mouth and glance at the time on the microwave. Lester will be here soon to pick me up for another date. I mentally roll my eyes. His parents are having a dinner party for his sister's birthday. I paid a visit to the mall and bought an appropriate outfit all on my own. The red satin knee-length dress is absolutely stunning. It's a relief his family and friends will be around to provide a barrier between us. Hopefully, he'll be too busy chatting with them to focus on me. I gasp, hearing the front door open.

"Who's there?" I step from the kitchen and see Dom.

It's obvious he's been in a fistfight. There's a cut above his right eyebrow and a bruise on his left cheek, and his top lip is split. He doesn't utter a single word, just watches me. His commanding presence magnifies the energy in the room. The unseen force caresses me, sending a bolt of electricity through my veins. Six days have passed since he stole my virginity, but it seems an eternity ago.

"What happened?"

"Nothing important." His gaze unhurriedly roams my body. "You look beautiful."

"Thank you," I say meekly.

"Hot date?"

"No, a friend invited me to a dinner party," I answer, hedging his stifling stare. I hate telling a half-truth, but Dom is too unpredictable, and I fear his reaction.

"Does Lester know he's just a friend?" he asks, smirking.

I jerk my eyes back to Dom. "How do you know about him?"

"I know everything."

"You've been stalking me."

He shrugs. "What is he to you?"

"It's complicated."

"Really," he says in a deathly soft tone, causing me to shiver.

"Can we talk later?" I have to get Dom out of here ASAP or risk him and Lester crossing paths.

"I'm hungry," he says, advancing towards me. "And thirsty."

"Dom, please." I backpedal into the kitchen.

"Feed me." He crowds me into the wall.

"I have to go."

"You're not going anywhere."

Dom snakes his hand under my dress and tears my panties off.

His blunt fingers explore my silken slit. "Wet for me already."

He grabs a glass cup from the dish rack and drops to his knees.

"What are you doing?" I ask, drawing in a sharp breath.

"First, satisfying my hunger. Then, I'll quench my thirst," he replies and positions the cup between my legs.

"I don't under—"

Dom buries his face at the crux of my thighs and French kisses my clit. I grip his blond mane and bring him closer, rotating my hips frantically. He hauls my right leg over his shoulder, then inserts two fingers inside my damp channel. A tingling sensation sparks to life and quickly intensifies. The levee breaks and fluid gushes from my opening. Convulsions rock me to the core, catapulting me into a flat spin towards solid ground. I shout, crash landing in a sea of flames. Dom rises to his feet, holding the now full glass. He drinks the milky liquid while peering into my eyes. The risqué act increases my sexual desire for him. Dom is the master of eroticism, a title well deserved.

"Have a taste." He tips the glass to my lips, and I greedily swallow the sweet elixir.

He puts the glass in the sink, then hoists me on top of the counter.

"We can't. Lester—"

"Fuck Lester," he snarls, undoing the closure of his jeans and freeing his erection.

"Not now, please."

"Your pussy is mine." He impales my pulsating sheath to the hilt, then holds steady as slight tremors rack his body. "And I'll take it whenever I want."

"You… you make me…" I'm at a loss as to how to describe the fever he stokes in me.

"It's a visceral reaction," he rasps thickly.

"What?"

"That's what you're experiencing. It's inherent… a compulsion that can't be explained. It just is."

"You said it wouldn't be like this all the time."

"It's not supposed to be," he says gutturally.

Dom hooks his arms underneath my knees and spreads me wide for his tantalizingly long strokes. I succumb to his devilish decadence, hopelessly ensnared by the potency of his sexuality. Our lips meet in a fervent kiss.

Tap tap tap.

Oh no… Lester.

"Let me answer," I plead. "I'll tell him I'm sick and can't go."

My request is met with silence.

The knock comes again. "Pepper?"

His pace doesn't falter, as if my "date" isn't outside my condo door waiting on me. My cell phone rings. I'm certain it's Lester trying to get ahold of me.

Dom carries me to the front door and bangs me against it so hard, my teeth clank together.

"Pepper, is that you?" Lester asks, jiggling the doorknob. "Are you okay?"

Dom locked it. Thank goodness for small favors. A prolonged inarticulate noise is torn from my throat as he bludgeons my tiny hole with ruthless thrusts. In the next instant, Dom throws open the door and unceremoniously dumps me on the floor at Lester's feet. He comes all over my hair and face.

"Pepper isn't available. She's too busy servicing my cock," he says silkily.

Lester's facial expression is comical, and if it weren't for the circumstances, I would laugh. Cum trickles down my nose and drips onto my lips. Embarrassed, I scoot backwards.

"Have a nice night." Dom shuts the door in his face.

"You… you fucking asshole!" I slap my hands across my mouth. I've never said a curse word in my life.

He smiles. "Damn, obscenities coming from you sound sexy as hell. Say more."

"Ugh!" I throw my arms up in frustration. "How could you do that?"

"You should be thanking me." He hefts me over his shoulder and walks towards my bedroom. "You don't even like him."

"Put me down!" I yell, squirming.

He whacks me on the bottom. "Stay still."

"My father is going to kill me."

Dom flings me onto the bed.

"Go before he gets here."

"Not a chance," he says, discarding his clothing. "I'm not done."

"For once, do what I ask!"

"I make the demands, not you." He gets on the bed and claws at my dress.

"This is a new dress!" I scream. "You can't keep ripping my clothes to shreds!"

"I'll buy you more."

I attempt to ward him off, but Dom promptly subdues me and mercilessly rams his manhood through my slick passage. He pumps into me so forcefully, the headboard strikes the wall in a sharp staccato, causing the wooden cross hanging above it to fall beside us. He plants his face in my neck, groaning hoarsely. Our fingers intertwine, seeking solace in each other as we careen towards pandemonium. The sheer violence of our joining spawns an unstoppable maelstrom destined to sever us in half. We're to blame for our destruction.

"I feel it too," Dom says gruffly.

"What?" I ask breathlessly.

"The visceral reaction of touching you... of fucking you. You torment me."

We orgasm as one, our impassioned cries resonating throughout the room.

CHAPTER 24

Dom

I fuck Pepper for the fourth time, plowing into her from behind at a rapid pace. One hand is used to secure her wrists at the center of her back, and the other presses her face into the mattress, stifling her pleas for me to stop. At this angle, her arch is accentuated and mobility is unattainable, allowing for maximum deepness. Rivulets of sweat stream down my body. She's hurting, but I can't stop fucking her. I'm hooked.

"You blasphemous whore!" Pepper's father appears in the doorway, clutching a Bible. I recognize him from stalking her.

I pull free of her, and she grabs the sheet to cover her nudity. "I can explain," Pepper says.

"You are a disgrace," he says in seething anger.

I spring out of bed, giving him a full-frontal view of my nakedness.

"White son of the devil!" he shouts in disgust. "You've tainted my daughter!"

"Son of the devil?" I ask, chuckling. "Oh no, I am the fucking devil."

"You're a vile man to corrupt an innocent girl!"

"I want to be with Dom and live life on my terms," Pepper cuts in. "You expecting me to marry Lester is a joke."

"You no longer have my financial support," he barks.

"Daddy—"

"Pack your belongings and leave this instant."

"No," she says firmly.

"Disobedient girl!" He barges into the room, lifting the Bible to strike Pepper.

I snatch the book from his grasp and bash him in the forehead with it, sending him tumbling to the floor. I prepare to thrash him again for good measure, but Pepper grabs my arm.

"Dom, don't."

"Raise a hand to her again, and no force on Heaven or earth will be able to save you from my fury."

"I'll have you arrested for assault," he threatens, clambering to his feet.

"If you do, the congregation will learn of your dirty little secret," Pepper says.

"What secret?"

"The child you fathered with your best friend's wife."

This scenario hits too close to home for me. Not long ago, I was on the receiving end of an unfaithful fiancée and backstabbing best friend.

"That is a lie."

"Patrick knows the truth too, and a simple DNA test will confirm it."

"You'd blackmail your own father for this white serpent?" he spits.

"And you'd destitute your own daughter. We're even."

"You're dead to me."

Her bravado falters, and sadness fills her eyes.

"Watch it," I growl, taking a step towards him.

He hastily backpedals.

She stiffens her resolve and pushes on. "I'm moving soon, but I expect you to continue paying for college."

He storms out of the condo in righteous indignation.

"This situation could've been prevented if you had let me talk to Lester," Pepper says in a voice thick with emotion. "Are you purposely aiming to sabotage my life?"

"I would've made sure you had a place to live and paid for school."

"And that exonerates your actions?"

"I don't regret what I've done."

"You're cold-blooded."

"As a fucking snake."

"Is this some sick twisted game to you? Please help me understand."

"It's not for you to understand."

"I care—"

"Enough, Pepper!" I boom. "Goddamn it! No more questions and no more trying to get inside my head!"

"I've never met a person more self-serving than you," she cries, lying on her side.

Shit, comforting a weeping female is a foreign concept to me.

I lie beside her and wipe her tears. "This is who I am. Accept it."

"I finally decided to control my own destiny and liberate myself from my father," she wails.

"Goal accomplished. What is the fucking problem?"

"It was supposed to be on my own terms, but you took the choice from me and made my victory hollow!"

"A victory is a triumph, no matter how it's obtained."

"You don't get it," she sobs. "After the hell he put me through as a child, I needed closure."

I gleaned some information about Pepper, but the particulars of her childhood are a mystery.

"What did he do?" The thought of anyone harming her makes my blood boil. It's convoluted given the fact I find pleasure in causing her pain, but no one is allowed to hurt her, *except me.* She guides my fingers along the underside of her left wrist. The skin is slightly scarred there. It's imperceptible, so I hadn't noticed before.

"You're not the only one who's been burned."

Pepper bawls her eyes out, recounting the sordid details of her upbringing, from the death of her mother and being homeschooled to recently learning of her half-sister. All of those events led to the life-altering decision to escape her father's rule. The story of her sperm donor holding her wrist over an open flame affected me the most. That motherfucker shouldn't be breathing. I want to rage but bite my tongue and listen to Pepper divulge horrific tales into the wee hours. Eventually, she falls asleep, fatigued and wrapped in my protective embrace.

Though Pepper went to sleep late, she woke with the sunrise. She stumbled to the bathroom, grumbling unhappily about cum in her hair and having to wash it. Once she's all clean, I'll take her to breakfast. I'm starving, and I'm sure she is too since neither of us ate dinner. I put my pants on and head to the kitchen in search of caffeine. I have a pot of coffee made in minutes and pour myself a huge cup. No sugar or cream added; I drink my java strong and black.

Before I can savor the flavor, there's loud banging on the front door. I slam the mug on the counter, spilling some of the hot brew on my hand.

"Goddamn it," I growl, walking to the door. "Who the fuck could that be at this time of morning?"

I look through the peephole and spot Pepper's brother. *He's probably here because of his father*, I muse, opening the door. His face scrunches in confusion, and he glances at the number on the door to verify he's at the correct location.

"I-is P-pepper h-home?" he asks, stuttering.

"She's in the shower," I answer, stepping back to allow him entry.

The shock wears off, and his eyes widen in recognition. "You're Dominic Stone."

"In the flesh." I go back into the kitchen, and he follows.

"Dude, you're rich and famous."

"I'm hardly a celebrity."

"Last year I had to write an essay about an entrepreneur who inspires me for my business class, and I chose you. You're one of the wealthiest self-made billionaires in the world."

Damn, an impressionable kid shouldn't see me as a role model. I'm a fucking asshole.

"My name is Patrick, by the way. I'm Pepper's brother."

"Good to meet you."

"Likewise." He grabs a carton of juice from the refrigerator and chugs down a big gulp.

I raise an eyebrow at him.

He smiles sheepishly. "Pepper buys fruit juice for me. She hates it."

I'm lucky I didn't drink any.

"I'm saving money for the Beacon Trinity. My father won't buy me one and refused to cosign for a monthly installment plan."

"It's the next step in the evolution of cell phones."

"The features are awesome. I can't wait to get one."

"How much do you have saved?"

"Two hundred so far."

"You have a long way to go."

"I'm picking up more hours at work." He polishes off the juice and tosses the carton into the garbage can. "Can I ask you a question?"

"Be my guest."

"Are you the reason my father came home yesterday ready to blow a gasket?"

"The one and only."

"I've never seen him that pissed."

"He'll get over it." I sip my coffee.

"Are you and my sister—"

"Patrick, what are you doing here?" Pepper scurries towards us, tying her robe.

"What the hell happened? Dad ranted and raved practically all night but wouldn't tell me anything."

"Dom, I need to talk to my brother, privately."

"I'll be in the shower," I say.

"There's a spare toothbrush, washcloth, and towel in the linen closet," she says.

I nod and amble down the hall.

CHAPTER 25

Pepper

Having a conversation with Patrick concerning my sex life will be a challenging endeavor. We settle on the sofa, but neither of us speaks. He picks invisible lint off his shirt, and I inspect my fingernails.

"Dad said I can never see or talk to you again," he says, ending the awkward silence.

"Is this goodbye?" I ask somberly.

Losing my brother would be a devastating blow for me.

"Hell no," he says, giving me a one-arm hug. "Screw him."

"He'll disown you too," I say, laying my head on his shoulder.

"Doesn't matter."

"Yes, it does. I won't be responsible for causing a rift between you and our father."

"I'm not enlisting in the military, remember? He'll disown me sooner or later anyway."

"I guess you're right, but let him believe you're obeying his orders for now at least. There's been enough drama."

"Fine." He regards me thoughtfully. "So, you're slapping uglies with your boss."

My cheeks heat. "He's not my boss."

"Well, he owns the company, so he kind of is, indirectly."

"Point taken."

Here comes the hard part.

"I know what I'm doing is wrong and a sin. I'm conflicted, but if I had the chance to undo it all, I wouldn't. Am I a bad person?"

"No, you're a person enjoying happiness for the first time in your life."

"You're wise beyond your years."

"Duh," he says smugly.

"You're so modest," I say sarcastically, punching him in the thigh.

"You're really into Freddy Krueger's twin brother, huh?" Patrick asks, laughing.

"Don't make fun of his appearance," I snap defensively.

"I'm sorry, Pepper," he says solemnly. "That was a terrible joke."

"Yeah, it was. Watch what you say about him."

"Okay. How serious is this?"

"I care about him a lot, but it's complicated."

"Why?"

I'm not explaining to my kid brother that Dom is only interested in a summer booty call.

"That's a discussion for another day."

"I'm surprised Dad allowed you to stay here."

"Well, he kind of didn't, exactly." I relay the blackmailing scheme to him.

"That's badass, Pepper."

Dom saunters into the living room fully dressed in yesterday's clothes.

"Get ready, we're going to breakfast," he says, towel-drying his hair. "Patrick, you're welcome to accompany us."

"I could always eat." He grins. "Thanks for inviting me."

"No problem."

"Dad will wonder why you're not in church."

"I'll handle him."

"But—"

"It'll be fine. Trust me."

"All right. Give me fifteen minutes," I say, heading to the bedroom.

"Yo, your ride is sick, dude!" Patrick shouts excitedly, running his hand along the sleek red paint. "One day, I'll be rich enough to afford a Ferrari Portofino convertible."

"You know your luxury vehicles," Dom says.

"I'm a car fanatic."

"Want to take it for a spin?"

"Are you shitting me?" he asks skeptically.

"Definitely not a good idea," I protest. "What if he totals your car?"

"Pepper, you're killing me." Patrick turns puppy-dog eyes on me. "I'm responsible for my age."

"I'll pay for any damages incurred." Dom winks at Patrick.

"Can I put the top down?"

"Knock yourself out."

"Sweet!" Patrick jumps into the driver's seat.

Dom slides into the passenger seat, and I climb in the back. "No speeding."

"Oh, I'm putting the pedal to the metal."

I flick his ear. "Hey, I mean it."

"Okeydoke, sis, no need to get your panties in a bunch."

"Whatever, just chill on the cowboy stunts."

"Record me driving." He hands me his cell phone. "My friends are going to freak."

"Will do, Your Highness," I say, starting the video.

Patrick starts the ignition. "Listen to that baby purr."

"Ease on the gas slowly," Dom says.

"Got it." He maneuvers into the flow of traffic.

"Do you know where Midnight Café is?"

"Yeah, I've been there before."

"That's our destination."

"Ten-four."

Dom isn't the awful person he has everyone believing he is. His generosity towards Patrick is confirmation. Not many people would trust a seventeen-year-old behind the wheel of their expensive car. Patrick's joviality is contagious, and I find myself beaming like a Cheshire cat despite my lack of faith in his driving abilities. My gaze collides with Dom's in the rearview mirror. My smile disappears at the potency in his amber depths. An elusive entity lurks there, awakening my desire. Some people underestimate the power of a look. In actuality, eyes are the windows to the soul and have the capability to make a person feel invincible, sexy, loved... but in the next instant evoke the opposite emotions, decimating a person's confidence. His is a punch to the gut. It raises my body temperature, accelerates my breathing, and causes liquid heat to spill onto my panties. He thoroughly penetrates my mind, psychologically making love to me. Patrick chatters nonstop, unaware of the shifting atmosphere. I should despise Dom. He takes without asking, demands without compromising, and offers no apology for his behavior. My life is in an uproar due to his actions, but to hate him is to hate myself. What a conundrum. Our mental connection grows stronger by the day. At summer's end, it'll be forged in steel. Dom will require a blowtorch to separate us, and when he succeeds, I'll be reduced to a catatonic state from which escape is futile. Half of him will be forever embedded in me. Maybe I'm distorting what we have into something it's not. Maybe this is infatuation… lust, as Dom said. Sex is new to me. Could it be I'm confusing the sentiments? Can love and lust not be mutually felt for the same person, or does one cancel out the other?

"Hellooooooo." Patrick's annoyed voice interrupts my inner dialogue.

"What?" I ask, a bit irritated.

"We're here." He regards Dom and me as if we've lost our marbles. "Are you two cool?"

"Of course, why?"

"We got here two minutes ago, but you guys haven't moved."

Dom remains quiet during Patrick's and my exchange.

"Oh, I hadn't noticed."

"Come on, I'm famished." Patrick gets out of the car and swiftly walks in the direction of the restaurant.

My eyes drift back to the rearview mirror. Dom still watches me, as I knew he would be. Unexpectedly, he latches on to the nape of my neck and hauls me forward for a kiss that holds dark promises.

"I'm going to feed your cunt so much cum, it'll seep through your fucking pores," he whispers against my lips.

Dang it, I love/lust him.

CHAPTER 26

Pepper

I recline sideways in a comfy chair inside the solarium, reading the book Jackie loaned me, and absentmindedly twirl my hair. There wasn't time to style my kinky locks, so a bushy ponytail had to suffice. After breakfast, Patrick drove back to my condo to pick up his car and went home. Dom took me to his mansion, and we made love—for the first time in his bedroom—into the early afternoon. We ate a late lunch of chicken salad sandwiches and mango on the terrace. Afterwards, Dom retired to his office to work, and I absconded here for solitude.

"What's poppin', girl?" Drew asks in his usual cheery voice.

I lay the book on my chest and crane my head towards the door. "Hi, just catching some R and R before the Monday morning rush."

"I hear that." He plops down in the chair opposite me. "Where's my knuckleheaded brother?"

"Working."

"On a Sunday!" Drew exclaims. "Gosh, he's a douchebag for abandoning a beautiful woman for crap that could be done tomorrow."

"We spent quality time together," I say, smiling shyly.

"Oh, did you now." He grins. "What'd you guys do?"

"Stop it, Drew."

"Sorry for teasing you, but you're an easy target." He laughs.

I really like Drew. Probably because he's the male version of Mia.

"Is Dom expecting you?"

"Nah, I had nothing better to do than come over and be a pain in his ass. It'll be the highlight of my Sunday."

I giggle. Yeah, he definitely has the Mia persona. "Must've been exciting in your household growing up."

"You have no idea."

"Your poor mother."

"Nonsense. The never-ending battles kept her young, and the antipsychotics the doctor prescribed kept her sane."

"I'm sure."

"Hopeless romantic?" he asks, pointing to the book.

"*Wuthering Heights* isn't a romance… it's a tragedy."

"Heathcliff and Cathy were passionately in love. Anyway, all romances end in tragedy."

"That's an interesting concept. Care to explain?"

"Okay, here's my perspective. One person has to die before the other, right? Eventually, an unforeseen obstacle will separate the couple, whether it be old age, an accident, illness, or something more sinister. It's inevitable. For example, the movie *Titanic*. Jack chose death to ensure Rose's survival. Also, there's *Romeo and Juliet*. The most famous star-crossed lovers in history met their end tragically."

"I acknowledge your theory has substance, but my stance on *Wuthering Heights* hasn't changed."

"That's your choice. I say it's an untraditional romance."

"They brought out the worst in each other."

"Love causes people to do crazy shit and makes fools of us all."

"You've read it from beginning to end?"

"Yeah, why?"

"Didn't peg you for the reading type."

"What's that supposed to mean?" he asks defensively.

"Oh, no… I only meant…"

His eyes twinkle with mirth.

"You're pulling my leg."

"I am." He guffaws. "Told ya… easy target."

"You got me, but I won't be so gullible next time."

"Challenge accepted." He winks. "You pegged me correctly. I only read *Wuthering Heights* because it was a requirement in my high school English class."

"To answer your question, yes, I am a hopeless romantic. Are you?"

"Hell yeah."

"You have a girlfriend?"

"Several, in fact."

"Figures."

"One woman can't handle all of this."

"Do you mean your gigantic head?"

"Why, yes… yes, I do."

"I was metaphorically speaking of your inflated ego," I deadpan.

"Oh, thought you were referring to something else." He chuckles.

"You're a modern-day Casanova, huh?"

"At your service."

"I fear for the female population."

"Women flock to me. Couldn't beat them off with a broom if I tried."

"You are by far the cockiest person in existence."

"Thanks for the compliment."

"You're so conceited." I laugh, finding bantering with Drew refreshing.

Dom

Pepper laughs boisterously at something Drew said. They haven't noticed I came into the damn room. My temper flares, and my inner beast bares its claws, ready to shred my brother to the bone. Drew swears he's a goddamn comedian. Sly bastard. It can't be that fucking funny.

"Am I interrupting?"

"Hey, bro, Pepper and I are shooting the breeze."

"Got everything done?" Pepper asks.

"Yes. Disappointed?"

"No," she says, confused. "Why would I be?"

"You seem to prefer my brother's company to mine. Should I give you and Drew some privacy?"

"What are you trying to imply?" Pepper asks.

"You two are flirting right under my fucking nose."

Drew jumps to his feet. "Dude, what's your problem?"

"We were having an innocent conversation," Pepper protests.

"Quit sniffing around Pepper."

"How could you think I'd betray you? I'm your fucking brother, Dom!" he shouts. "I'm not to blame for your best friend fucking your fiancée." He storms from the room.

"Your best friend? Why didn't you tell me? Knowing helps me understand you better."

"Don't start your psychobabble!" I bellow, leaving the solarium in search of Drew. He would never break my trust. It's Pepper. I'm a raging lunatic because of her. I spot him and quickly match his stride.

"I'm an asshole."

"Some apology," he snorts, facing me.

"It's all you're getting."

"Jealousy turns you into an even bigger turd."

"I'm not jealous," I deny.

"Pepper has you tied in knots. You're a goner, admit it."

"She's a summer fling."

"You're using her?" he asks in disgust. "That's low."

"She knows what this is. I've been straightforward from the beginning."

"I was rooting for you and her, but now I hope she kicks your pathetic ass to the fucking curb. Pepper deserves a man who'll cherish her."

"Prince Charming will have to wait until summer's over. Until then, she belongs to me."

"I'm outta here." He throws his hands up in annoyance. "You're a major dick."

I barge back into the solarium, startling Pepper. "Go to my bedroom."

"We should talk," she says tensely, eyes wide as saucers.

"No talking, only fucking," I say softly, but there's no mistaking the underlying threat.

"It isn't fair—"

"Obey on your own accord, or I'll drag your ass there. Either option concludes with my cock buried in your cunt."

She slowly stands and walks through the door. I'll alleviate my frustrations between her thighs.

Pepper

Lisa was supposed to meet me at the ice cream parlor a half hour ago, but I don't mind waiting. It gives me time to rehash the events of the past week. Dom and I haven't spent the lunch hour together much since he's busy with negotiations to expand Stone Inc. However, we've spent every night together. He's in denial, but the dynamics of our "relationship" have changed, and I couldn't be more ecstatic. His sour attitude does dampen my happiness a little. I wish he would stop fighting this and give us a chance.

"Hi, Pepper!" Lisa approaches me, waving excitedly.

"Hey, you look really pretty." Her tie-dye romper and oversized sunglasses are stylish. The hip-length braids she's sporting complement her chic attire. She's a carefree teenager. Something I never had the chance to be.

Lisa twirls around, then strikes a pose. "Thank you."

I smile, adoring her sassy attitude.

She hops onto the stool. "I love this place. They have the best rocky road ice cream, and it's made in the shop," she gushes.

"Is that what you want? It's on me."

"Oh yeah, the mega size, please."

"Coming right up."

I order at the counter and return to the table with our cold treats.

"Much appreciated, sis."

"You know?" I say, astonished.

"That your dad is banging my mom and we're sisters? Yep," she says, stuffing a spoonful of the chocolate concoction into her mouth.

"When did you find out?"

"A year ago. My mother's sneaky behavior went unnoticed by my father, but not me. He's a bit of a space cadet."

"And you kept it to yourself."

"My mom swore me to secrecy, but she can go fall off a cliff for all I care. I keep quiet for my dad's sake. How long have you known?"

"Few weeks."

"Figured you knew since you invited me to hang out of all of a sudden. Does Patrick know?"

"He's the one who told me."

"Neither of you blabbed," Lisa states.

"For the same reason as you, to protect others."

I can't say "Oh, and I'm blackmailing our father." Had he called my bluff; he would've won. Though I have the key to Pandora's box, I wouldn't have opened it. I just needed a place to live and to finish college. If that meant resorting to underhanded methods, so be it. The secret will be revealed one day, but not by me.

"There's already a scandal circulating through the church anyway." Lisa winks. "Don't need another one."

"What scandal?"

"You, silly."

"Me?"

"Yeah, it's common knowledge you're boinking a white man. The consensus is you're a very bad, bad, naughty girl."

"Jesus."

"Is that who you call out to when you're doing the nasty?" Lisa asks saucily.

Her sassiness is not welcome at the moment.

"What's being said?"

Lester definitely let the cat out of the bag, because my father would've taken this to the grave. He'd be too embarrassed to confide in anyone.

"Lester wasn't in church on Sunday, and rumor has it, he isn't coming back. The reason why spread through the congregation like wildfire. No exact details were given. Your father was livid."

Patrick is clueless to all of this or else he would've relayed it to me. He missed church last week, but I'm surprised Dad didn't mention anything to him.

"I'll be considered a leper among the members now."

"Who cares? They're a bunch of old, stuffy, judgmental sons of bitches."

While Lisa devours her ice cream, mine is left melting and forgotten. I'm not in the mood for it anymore.

"Who's the guy?" she asks.

"That's private."

"You can trust me."

"Lisa, I'm not telling you," I say sternly to stop her from pressing the issue.

"Okay," she replies, crestfallen. "Do you regret coming?"

"No, absolutely not. Despite the circumstances, I'm thrilled to have a sister."

"I always hated being an only child and remember constantly wishing on shooting stars for a sister. Having a brother too is a bonus."

"I'll plan a day for the three of us to spend together."

"That would be so awesome."

We chat a little longer before promising to see each other again and leaving. I dial Patrick on the drive home.

"Hello."

"Hey, what are you up to?"

"Just got to work."

"I'll give you a ring later, then."

"I have fifteen minutes to spare."

I recount the conversation Lisa and I had in full detail, answering his questions if further clarification was needed.

"That's why he's been in a shitty mood all week and barely spoken two words to me," Patrick says.

"It'll be hard for him to save face."

"It's time for the perfect façade he's built to come crashing down anyway."

"You'll be smack-dab in the middle of the church drama tomorrow."

"I have to clock in, but don't worry about me. I can handle it."

"Okay. Call if you need me."

"Wait a sec. Can you text me Dominic's cell?"

"What for?"

"To thank him for the Beacon Trinity."

"He gave you a cell phone?"

"Yeah, assumed you knew. It came in the mail yesterday."

"No, he didn't say anything."

"Gotta go. Send the number. Bye."

As suspected, the devil has a heart of gold.

CHAPTER 28

Pepper

"Sunrise Plaza or Chaplin Ridge?" I ask, staring at Mia's animated features on my cell phone.

We need to find a place to live, but Mia's diva complex is making it beyond difficult. She's vetoed a dozen apartments. My rear end is numb from sitting at the table for so long.

"It's superhard to choose," she whines, poking out her bottom lip.

"We'll end up homeless if you don't quit being picky," I chide.

"Which one has the washer and dryer inside the unit?" she asks.

"Chaplin."

"And the other one has the walk-in closet and dishwasher?"

"Yep, and both have swimming pools."

"I've always dreamed of having a walk-in closet." She sighs. "But I need the convenience of a washer and dryer."

"At Sunrise, the laundry room is on the ground level of the building. May not be in the apartment but still convenient."

"I'm too lazy to go all the way down there," Mia grumbles.

"Keep in mind, these apartments will not be on the market forever, and we need to move in by August." Her indecision is giving me whiplash.

"Fine. Sunrise it is."

"Great. I'll call the leasing consultant on Monday."

"Okay, on to more fun topics. I've created an itinerary for your visit."

"I'm very afraid."

"You should be."

"Let me hear it."

"Nope, it's a surprise."

"I can't believe I'll be twenty-one in two weeks."

"What time does your flight get in?"

"Eight thirty in the morning."

"Bish, you ain't getting no sleep during your visit because we're partying day and night!" Mia stands and twerks in front of the camera, giving me a full view of her thong-clad buttocks.

"Please stop."

"You're just jelly of my big phat booty."

"We both know I have way more in the trunk than you do."

"Did you have to rain on my parade?" Thankfully, the butt shaking ceases, and she deposits it in the chair. "For your info, I've been doing five hundred squats a day."

"Uh-huh."

"Anyway, are you seeing Daddy Dom tonight?"

"For the hundredth time, lose *Daddy*." I had no idea what the term meant until Mia educated me.

Ever since telling her the Lester and blackmailing story, she won't relinquish this stupid moniker.

"You're the boss," Mia says cheekily. She agreed too easily for my liking. "I bet Sugar Daddy Dom is going to buy you something big and lavish for your b-day."

Great. She'll drop it if I pretend the new nickname doesn't bother me. "I didn't mention my birthday to him."

"Why?"

"He's not obligated to buy me a present."

The last thing I want from Dom is money and gifts. He thinks all women are after him for monetary gain. My goal is to prove him wrong. It's the reason why I kept my birthday under wraps. Avoiding sending him the wrong message is a priority to me.

"Sweetie, you're fucking a billionaire, and turning twenty-one is a huge milestone."

"It isn't important to me."

"Whatever, Ms. Goody Two-shoes." Mia gives me the stank face she's expertly perfected.

That's my cue to go before her trash-talking escalates. "I need to hop in the shower."

"Getting your kitty cat all spick-and-span for some licking and sticking." She sticks out her tongue and goes Linda Blair in *The Exorcist* on me.

"Bye, Mia." I end the video chat.

I wonder where Dom is. He left this morning and said he'd be back later, but it's close to six now. Maybe he changed his mind. I go into the bathroom and undress. After my shower, I'll shoot him a text. I lather myself using my favorite soap, then rinse off.

The shower curtain is snatched open, and I scream bloody murder until my eyes focus on Dom.

"You scared me to death!" I shout, twisting the valve off and stepping out of the bathtub.

He hands me my robe. "I have an early birthday surprise for you."

"You do?" I ask, dumbfounded.

"Unfortunately, I'll be at Lake Arrowhead on your birthday, but I'm cutting my trip short and driving home Sunday. I'll have another surprise for you then."

"I leave for Denver on my birthday," I say, donning my robe. "I'll be gone for a week. Can we reschedule?"

"Is there a reason why you haven't mentioned this before?" he asks, clearly angry. This is my first time hearing of his trip, but I'm not upset.

"Figured you wouldn't care."

"Visiting someone special?"

"Yeah, my friend Mia. She plans on taking me to all the nightclubs and—"

In a flash, Dom's large hand covers my face, and I'm thrown against the wall. The jarring collision rattles my brain and knocks the breath from me. His palm shields my nose and mouth, obstructing the flow of oxygen.

"You're going to stay here and wait for me," he snarls.

I earnestly grapple to extricate myself as my deprived lungs burn and panic sets in.

"What you'll be hitting is my pelvic bone while I'm splitting your pussy open doggy-style." His hand slips from my face, and I inhale a big gulp of air.

"Do you understand me?" he asks menacingly, pressing his nose to mine.

I nod my head jerkily, afraid of what he'll do if I refuse to concede.

"Say the fucking words."

"I understand," I wheeze.

He grabs my wrist and tugs me down the hallway.

"I have to get dressed."

"That isn't necessary."

"I can't go anywhere in my robe." He exits my condo, towing me along, and strolls into my neighbor's place like it's his residence.

"What the heck are we doing in here?"

Dom tugs me into the bedroom. A man holding a video camera hovers in the corner. Julian and Kaci lie on the bed, completely unclothed. I assume it's her. Finally, I can put a face to the woman whose passionate cries I've heard for the last several months. Her lithe figure and silky blond hair are stunning. They're an alluring picture.

"What is this?" I ask breathlessly.

"Your fantasy," Dom answers, untying my sash. "They're yours to command."

A passage in my diary outlines my desire to witness the pair having sex. Dom is bringing my vision to fruition.

"I can't," I say, holding the lapels together. My nipples stiffen and my center pulsates, contradicting my negative response. Watching Kaci lovingly stroke Julian's length and hearing the sexual noises he emits amplifies my hunger.

"You yearn for this." Dom tears my robe off and ushers me into a chair situated at the side of the bed. "This will be our secret. They all signed a nondisclosure agreement and will be handsomely compensated."

"Why are you having this taped?"

"So you can have a keepsake."

I cross my arms self-consciously. A thousand thoughts bombard me. I silence them and drag in a fortifying breath to calm my rioting nerves.

"They await your instructions," he presses.

Dom's formidable presence at my back goads me on.

"T-touch h-her b-breasts," I stutter.

Julian speedily responds, massaging Kaci's perky mounds. She mewls, basking in his caresses. This prompts the cameraman into action. He nimbly bustles about the area, recording the sensual sights.

Dom gives my swollen bosom the same treatment, kneading the sensitive flesh.

"Rub your clit," I demand fervently, remarkably in a strong, audible tone, becoming bolder.

Kaci spreads her legs and indulges my whim. From this vantage point, I'm granted an unimpeded view of her glistening pink vulva. Her hips gyrate as her fingers work feverishly. Dom walks around the chair and kneels between my thighs.

"Your pussy is an exemplary treasure." He leisurely licks from my slit to my nub, where he lingers, using his brilliant tongue to circle the heart of my pleasure.

Kaci thrashes, crying out as she achieves climax. Within seconds, I join her in carnal gratification. Once my tremors dissipate, Dom rises to his feet.

"Fuck her." The derogatory expletive effortlessly slips from my lips, my propriety forgotten.

"That's my slutty girl," Dom praises.

Julian poises himself on top of his sweetheart.

"No, from behind," I say.

He maneuvers Kaci to her knees and ruthlessly plunges into her.

"Yes, baby!" she wails. "Your dick is fucking amazing!"

Kaci's kudos spur him on. I'm enraptured, gazing at his manhood—now covered in her white cream—stretching the supple walls of her sheath.

Dom unbuttons the closure of his jeans and extricates his bulging erection, then pulls me to my feet and replaces me in the chair.

"Sit on my cock."

I face the bed and guide his thickness inside my wet depths, my eyes never wavering from the sexy duo. Dom digs his long fingers into my fleshy waist and plants kisses on the nape of my neck. My small passage strains to accommodate his girth from this position.

"You can't fit," I whimper.

He brutishly pulls me downwards, wholly spearing my overtaxed muscles in one deft movement. The savageness of his intrusion temporarily paralyzes me.

"Fuck, fuck, fuck," Dom chants, burying his face between my shoulder blades.

I clasp on to his sturdy thighs for support and rotate my hips, emancipating my wanton alter ego.

Dom's skilled fingers tweak my nipple and strum my clit, stimulating my nerve endings to astounding heights.

"Fuck her like she's your enemy, Julian," I say huskily, reveling in my kinky side.

The ferocity of his thrusts intensifies, and she unleashes a screeching cry.

"What's in your fucking pussy, Pepper? It's too damn good," Dom whispers in my ear. "The most addictive I've ever had."

"Shit, I'm about to come!" Julian bellows.

My core spasms, and a torrent of hot liquid streams from my opening. "Dom! It's too much!"

A collection of grunts and shouts fill the room, producing an erotic melody. This is the best birthday present I've ever received.

CHAPTER 29

Pepper

I lift my heavy suitcase off the conveyor belt and apprehensively scan the airport, certain a pissed-off Dom would appear and drag me back to California. Assured the coast is clear, I head to the exit. Disobeying him wasn't an easy decision, but I couldn't miss this trip. My flight was booked a while ago, and Mia is more ecstatic about my twenty-first birthday than I am. I packed after he left for Lake Arrowhead yesterday evening. He called at midnight to wish me a happy birthday. Maintaining my composure during the conversation was a true test of my fortitude. My guilty conscience almost had me blurting my intentions. Hopefully, upon my return, his temper will have cooled. If not, well…

I push through the glass door. It's a beautiful, mild day in Denver; a welcome break from the sweltering humidity of the Golden State.

"My little voyeur!" I smile hearing Mia's familiar voice.

She races towards me and launches herself into my arms. We embrace each other tightly. I called her while waiting to board the plane and described in detail Dom's birthday gift to me. Of course she asked a zillion questions and demanded to see the video, to which I said *"There's no way on God's green earth I'll ever let you watch it."*

"I'm so happy you're here." She releases me and peers over her shoulder. "Come on, Marco."

"I'm coming, bitch," he huffs. "Walking in four-inch heels isn't easy."

"You shouldn't have worn those damn shoes," Mia retorts.

"Quit your complaining. It's important I look fab at all times."

This is the infamous Marco. He and Mia became friends in high school. I've heard all about him but never had the pleasure of an introduction. The tall Italian wasn't in town during my visit the previous summer. He's positively marvelous in his silver sequined belly shirt, hot pink booty shorts, and matching pumps. Marco's short hair mirrors all the colors of the rainbow, and his makeup is flawless.

"Happy born day," he says jovially, giving me a hug.

"Thanks. It's good to finally meet you."

"Ditto, honey." He steps back and peruses me from top to bottom, rubbing his chin thoughtfully. "Your makeover is going to be *Next Top Model* worthy."

"Makeover?" I ask, eyeing them warily.

"Relax, you're overdue for a different look," Mia says. "The upgraded Pepper debuts tonight."

"What's on the agenda?"

"Marco got us an eleven o'clock appointment at his sister's salon for hair and nails. Then we're shopping for the skankiest dresses ever designed and stripper stilettos. Lastly, I'm throwing you a pre-celebration party at my house before heading to the club. We're painting the town red tonight, baby."

"I'm in charge of makeup," Marco chimes in. "I have the perfect color scheme in mind for your lovely complexion."

I purse my lips together.

"Lose the sour face, Pepper. You were a bore last year and stayed in most nights. That's not happening again."

"I went out."

"Yeah, to the flea market with my mom and grandmother. Thank heavens my parents and grandparents are on a cruise."

Marco explodes into boisterous laughter.

"The bargains there were awesome. We should all go."

"Bite your tongue," Mia gasps.

"Is she joking?" Marco asks, perplexed.

"I'm afraid not." Mia shakes her head. "Pepper, you're a lost cause."

"Darling, you'll be solo on that excursion," Marco says.

"Okay, people, we need to hustle. Breakfast, then off to be glamorized."

"Great, I'm starving," I say.

We settle into Marco's SUV and head to our first destination.

I'm exhausted after waking at the crack of dawn and spending the earlier part of today in transformation. The end result was worth the hassle. I regard the new me in the full-length mirror in the guest bedroom. I'm unrecognizable. A tiara graces the top of my head. My usual curly hair is straight for the first time in my life. The silken strands flow to the middle of my back. I absolutely love the bangs the stylist cut. The black strapless latex mini dress emphasizes my womanly assets. A "Happy Birthday" sash lies across my torso. Underneath the skimpy attire is a flimsy thong. Transparent platform heels complete the ensemble. Marco is an exemplary makeup artist. Foundation, concealer, eyeshadow, blush, eyeliner, and mascara contour my appearance. The shimmery silver hue Marco applied on my eyelids and the bright red lipstick really draw attention. I regard my long coffin-shaped acrylic nails. Completing the simplest chore is daunting with these things.

"Done ogling yourself?" Mia asks, leaning on the doorjamb.

She looks incredible in a white lace corset top, short turquoise skater skirt, and shoes similar to my own. Her long locks were cut and styled into a bob.

"I can't believe this is me."

"You're smoking hot. Hell, I'd fuck you if I were a lesbian."

I feel daring and sexy. If my father saw me, he'd have a conniption.

"Get your butt downstairs. Everyone is waiting on you."

Trepidation assails me. I heard the constant ringing of the doorbell. "Who are all those people?"

"Friends I've known for years."

"They're strangers to me."

"I'll introduce you. We'll socialize a bit before leaving for the club."

"Are they coming too?"

"Yep and the hot neighbor I told you about is tagging along."

"Mia, no matchmaking plots."

"You got it." Her green eyes sparkle in mischief.

"I'm serious."

"Sure, now come on."

We enter the family room where a dozen or so people mingle. Lavender and royal blue decorations adorn the space—my favorite colors. A bouquet of balloons floats near a table filled with hors d'oeuvres and cupcakes. Swirl pieces hang from the ceiling, and a birthday banner is taped to the wall. The Martha Stewart in Mia came to the forefront. She truly outdid herself. My eyes mist. I never had a noteworthy celebration on the date of my birth.

"No crying, you'll mess up your makeup."

"Thank you so much for this."

"Welcome, babe." Mia whistles. "All eyes on me!"

The chatter stops, and I become the center of attention. The shyness in me recoils at being thrown in the spotlight.

"This is the birthday girl, Pepper. All of you motherfuckers better be extra nice to her, or I'm whooping asses."

A chorus of "happy birthday" greets me. Mia points to each person and supplies their name and then conversations resume.

Dom

Drew and I were at each other's throats all day. His vocal dismay of my liaison with Pepper grated on my goddamn nerves. Our exchange of words escalated to physical blows on the fishing boat. Jensen tried unsuccessfully to separate us, and we all fell into the lake. In the fray, the fish we spent hours accumulating, and the bait, were lost. When we got back to the cabin, Drew shut himself in his room, and I've been nursing a beer on the porch swing.

Jensen ambles outside. "Mind if I join you?"

"Yes, I do."

He ignores me and plops his ass in the space next to me. "You're more temperamental than usual since Pepper came into your life."

I can't deny the truth of Jensen's statement. "Discussions involving her are off-limits."

"I didn't come out here to argue. Talk to me. I haven't been the best big brother, but you can confide in me."

"I have nothing to say."

"You've never acted this way over a woman before. Not even Lauren."

"Save your opinion."

He sighs in annoyance. "Drew told me everything. You won't be able to walk away from her, and you're fooling yourself if you think otherwise."

"You'll be proven wrong."

"I see what you refuse to."

I peer at him. "Which is?"

"You're in love." Jensen drops his two cents and goes back inside.

He's mistaken. I'm in lust and possessive of her but definitely not in love. I head to my room to check my cell for any missed calls or texts from Pepper. Seeing there are none, I give her a ring, but she doesn't answer. I access her condo's video feed. It's empty and dark. I call a second time and get her voicemail again. Where the fuck is she? In seconds, Pepper's location is pinpointed through the GPS chip I installed in her phone. Something in me snaps. I'm on a warpath, my destination... Denver.

Pepper

I'm a wretch for ignoring Dom but couldn't chance him hearing the noise in the background. I'll return his call when it's quiet and I'm alone. Grant, Mia's sexy new neighbor, and I gyrate to the music on the dance floor. My feet ache, but I'm having the time of my life. We hit it off at the house. He's charming and funny. I would be into him if my heart wasn't set on Dom. Grant grasps my hips and brings me closer. I'm tipsy, bordering on drunk. The alcohol Mia convinced me to consume vanquished my insecurities. A sudden chill envelops me, prickling my skin. Someone is watching me. The foreboding is so thick, it tightens my chest, suffocating me. Danger is imminent. I step away from my partner and hastily survey the dimly lit building, searching for the unknown threat.

"Are you okay?" Grant asks.

"I have to go."

"Why?" Confusion is evident in his tone.

"I'm sorry."

I push through the swarm of clubgoers, needing to flee the invisible menace closing in on me. I stop dead in my tracks, spotting a figure silhouetted in darkness directly ahead of me. There he is. My phantom in the flesh. *Dom*. Though his face is hidden in shadows, I have no doubt it's him. If I were blindfolded in a room full of people, I'd single him out. His energy will forever draw me to him. My surroundings fade, ceasing to exist. It's just him and me. Running and hiding is senseless. He'll capture me and seek retribution for my insubordination. It's better for me to accept the inevitable. I move forward until the tips of my breasts brush against him. Outwardly, he appears calm, but the wrath in his eyes belies that notion. He turns on his heel and walks towards the exit. I quietly follow. The street is mostly empty, save for a few inebriated stragglers. My footwear prohibits me from matching Dom's long strides.

"How did you find me?" My question is met with silence. "I had to come."

In the blink of an eye, Dom grabs my hair and drags me down a nearby alley. He flings me onto the worn pavement. I flip to my bottom and scuttle backwards. My palms and knees are scraped raw, absorbing the brunt of the fall.

"What are you going to do?"

He undoes his belt buckle and pulls the thick black band from the loops. Oh my God. He's going to beat me.

"Somebody help me! He's crazy!" I yell, crawling away.

He lies on top of me and wraps the strap around my throat, strangling me. I twist and wiggle, but he's too heavy to dislodge. Dom pushes my face into the small puddle of water formed by a pit in the concrete. Surely, I won't meet my demise at such a young age. I pray, asking God to spare me. Suddenly, Dom's oppressive weight disappears. I roll over, coughing and gasping for breath. A stranger came to my rescue, but Dom pummels the poor soul in a psychotic rage. I look on, horrified at the display of savagery. This man will die because of me.

"Stop!" I shout.

An uppercut sends my champion crumpling to the cement. He doesn't move. Oh no. Is he dead? Dom lifts the motionless man and throws him into the dumpster, then shuts the lid. I get up and stumble down the alley, but a barrier blocks my escape.

"There's nowhere to go, Pepper," Dom taunts. "Scream for help again. I'll drop your next hero and toss him into the garbage too."

Desperate, I latch on to the chain-link fence and climb.

Dom laughs maniacally. "You're right to be afraid."

He takes ahold of the belt still firmly secured around my neck and gives a sharp tug. I crash onto the ground.

"I'll never disobey you again," I weep, my stomach churning in fear.

I'm hauled to my feet and thrown against the steel wire. "Pull your dress up, then hold on to the fence."

I expose my backside and place my hands where directed.

"Phenomenal," he says in reverence, tracing the waistband of my thong. "Did you wear these for the motherfucker you were dancing with?"

"No. I swear."

"You're due for an ass whooping. Twenty-one strikes is fitting for your disobedience." His palm cracks across my rear end, jolting me. "Count."

"Please don't do this!" I wail, tears streaming from my eyes.

"I said, fucking count!" he bellows.

"One," I sob.

He delivers another agonizing hit.

"Two."

Nineteen to go. My body convulses from the stinging slaps—each one harder, more excruciating than the last. Finally, my harrowing punishment is over.

"I hope you learned a valuable lesson," he says, fondling my sore buttocks.

"I did," I croak.

"Good." He unzips his fly. "Listening to your anguished screams made me so damn horny, I nearly came in my boxers." His lips graze the shell of my ear.

"I need to rest," I say, fatigued and emotionally drained.

"And I need to fuck." Dom pulls my thong to the side and violently thrusts inside me. "Your pussy is dripping wet and so fucking hot."

"It hurts," I whisper.

"It's supposed to," he grunts.

His right hand grips the fence for purchase, and the left fastens around the belt, once again cutting off precious air. Dom callously batters between my thighs, not showing an ounce of leniency. My garbled cries echo through the night. I'm on the verge of losing consciousness.

"Did you think I wouldn't come for you?" he growls. "Never underestimate me."

With lighting speed, Dom changes positions, pinning me to the brick wall. My legs circle his waist as he continues pillaging my tight sheath. His teeth sink into my shoulder, piercing my flesh and marking me in the most primal way. My muscles contract, responding to his wild and brutal claiming. A torrent of spasms rocks my center, shattering me into a million pieces. Dom groans, bulldozing in and out of me like a madman. We ride the high of our orgasm together and then he carries me to his car.

CHAPTER 31

Dom

I spot Pepper strolling along the beach from the kitchen window. She's fucking gorgeous. Her glossy mane and gold nightgown billow in the wind, lending her an ethereal quality. After waking in bed alone, I donned my boxer briefs and went to search for her. We arrived at my private island two days ago for a week's stay—my other birthday gift to her. I drove to her friend's house and ordered her to pack her shit and be back outside in five minutes. Pepper was livid but followed my instructions. She's showing her displeasure by scarcely speaking to me. Honestly, she's doing me a favor. A quiet woman is preferable to a whining, nagging one. The moment my eyes locked on her in the club, an uncontrollable bloodlust consumed me, and she suffered for it. That scrap of cloth considered a dress barely covered her ass, and the tiny thong underneath it left her pussy lips exposed. They will be added to my "Pepper's panties" collection. And those sexy as fuck heels, my God… she wore them while I fucked her senseless last night. I admit my behavior is irredeemable… atrocious, but I can't bring myself to care. I'm a remorseless Grade-A asshole.

My stomach growls, reminding me to eat breakfast. My caretaker brought food and toiletries for our stay. I scan the contents of the refrigerator to decide this morning's menu. It doesn't take long to whip up a meal. I set a spread of western omelets, toast, butter, orange juice, and coffee on the table. Pepper comes into the kitchen, glaring at me.

"Hungry?" I ask, sweetly.

"Yes," she answers sharply and sits in the chair adjacent to me.

She eats a piece of her omelet and frowns, not impressed with my culinary skills.

"Something wrong?"

"It's bland," she says snidely.

The silent treatment isn't bothering me, so she's trying a different angle to test my patience, but I relish a challenge.

"I know just what's needed." I stand and pull out my cock.

"I'm confused," she says.

"Obviously, I mean for you to suck it."

She rebelliously shakes her head.

"Tsk, tsk, tsk." I seize her sleek tresses in a vise hold, snatching strands from her scalp. "Open. Your. Mouth."

She grimaces in pain and hastily complies. I surge forward, hammering her tonsils relentlessly. Pepper retches, inept to handle the ruthless onslaught. In a desperate bid for freedom, her fingernails score my abdomen. After a few more strokes, I draw back and come on her omelet.

"Enjoy."

"I lost my appetite."

"Eat."

"No." She seals her lips.

I'm not sure what caused this new defiant attitude, but it's invigorating.

"I'll assist you."

Pepper moves her head from side to side, but I manage to pry her jaw open and force a forkful of egg into her mouth.

"Swallow." I cover the bottom half of her face, forcing compliance.

Before I can feed Pepper another serving, she hurls the plate onto the floor.

I haul her across the table and rip her panties off. "You need to be reminded of who's in charge."

"Fuck you!" she screams.

"You're becoming a very naughty girl," I say, slathering warm butter on my length.

"Kiss my ass!"

"I'd rather fuck you in the ass." I position my erection at the cleft of her lovely cheeks and push into her muscular ring.

"No, not there. Please!" she cries frantically.

"Where has your bravado gone?"

"Oh God, stop! You're too big!"

The virgin orifice is so snug it's difficult to fit my breadth inside. I give a mighty thrust, filling her rectum to the brim. She lets out a loud, keening cry. Shit, the death grip on my cock is fucking nirvana.

"Shh, it's okay," I murmur, tearing through her puckered hole hard and fast.

She grabs the fork and stabs me in my left hand.

"Goddamn it!" I thunder, infuriated.

The minuscule wounds bleed profusely. Pepper uses the distraction to make a run for it. I promptly chase her down, wrestle her against the stove, and ram my dick back into her tender flesh at rapid speed.

"There's nowhere on this island you can hide from me." I delve my bloody fingers between her velvet soft folds and penetrate her sweet warm haven.

Pepper's distressed sobs evolve to high-pitched moans of ecstasy, and her body writhes uncontrollably. I meet her in orgasmic satisfaction moments later.

I hoist her over my shoulder. "It's time for a shower."

Pepper

The glowing full moon illuminates the vast crystal-clear blue ocean. The opulent villa is the stuff of fairy tales. Under different circumstances, I could appreciate its beauty. My feet sink into the squishy white sand as I traipse down the coast. I came outside a while ago to listen to the rolling waves. The rhythmic sound calms my rampaging emotions. The last forty-eight hours have been a whirlwind. Mia gave me an earful about my abrupt departure from Denver. To get in her good graces, I agreed to the occasional party at our new apartment.

Dom is a whole other story. We spent the better part of the day fighting and having sex, leaving my nether regions severely chafed. He confessed to installing hidden cameras in my condo but wouldn't reveal the exact location of the devices. The thought of him watching me in the bathroom is mortifying. My only consolation is his confirmation that none would be installed at my new apartment since I'll have a roommate. To add further insult to injury, he also planted a GPS chip in my cell phone, which he blatantly refuses to remove. Dom acts as if he has every right to invade my privacy. Regardless of everything he's done, I feel awful for stabbing him. He had me clean and wrap the small punctures instead of seeking medical attention on the mainland.

"This is the second time today I woke in bed alone." Dom, in all his naked glory, appears at my side.

"The ocean is peaceful."

He slips the negligee down my arms, revealing my nudity. "Up for a dip?"

"Yeah."

We wade into the lukewarm swell. Feeling playful, I splash water in Dom's face. In retaliation, he dunks me under the surface. Far from deterred, I douse him again and hastily swim out of his reach. Dom, not one to be bested, quickly pursues me.

"Your ass is mine."

"Ha! You're too slow to catch me," I boast.

He latches on to my ankle and drags me to him.

"Eek!" I screech.

"You were saying?" he asks, lifting me above his head.

"Don't you dare!"

He throws me into the sea. I come up sputtering and coughing. He laughs boisterously at my plight, but seeing him happy and carefree is a breath of fresh air. We swim back to the shore and lie on the beach.

"Mind if I ask a question?"

"You can, doesn't mean I'll answer it."

"Why don't you want to have children?"

"Never said I didn't."

"But you had a vasectomy."

"Which is reversible."

"So, you plan to tie the knot one day?"

"Yes."

"Even though you don't believe in love."

"A wife and children are necessary to carry on my legacy."

"Basically, your marriage will be a loveless business arrangement."

"Correct."

"How will you find this woman? I doubt advertising in the local newspaper is an option."

"Enough questions," he snaps. "Go inside and start dinner."

I figured my questions would kill the mood, but I was too curious not to ask.

"No child should grow up in a loveless household," I say before heading inside.

CHAPTER 32

Pepper

Loud rock 'n' roll pierces my sleep-muddled brain. I roll to my stomach, groaning in annoyance, and bury my head beneath the comforter.

"Wake up, sleepyhead," Mia singsongs, entering my bedroom, then snatching the comforter from me.

We finally moved into our apartment last weekend, and since then, she's been a pain in my butt.

"Ugh." I flip onto my back. "Please turn the volume down."

Mia is already showered and dressed, looking trendy in a white crop top and pineapple-print shorts.

She claps her hands. "Up and at 'em."

"What time is it?" I whine, not at all pleased at being woken in this manner.

"Ten."

"Have you lost your ever-loving mind?" I grab a pillow and throw it at her, which she promptly dodges.

"Yeah. You know I'm a crazy bitch."

"Out," I order.

"Uh-uh." Mia clucks her tongue. "We're going shopping for the party tonight."

"Why do I have to go?"

"You ditched me in Denver, and all I ask—"

"Okay, okay," I grumble, interrupting her tirade. "I'll go."

"Awesome saucesome." She does a little dance. "Get ready, we leave in thirty."

"Caffeine?" I ask, yawning and stretching.

"Yep, I'll grab you a cup, sweetcakes," she says, bounding from the room.

It's too early for her to be so freaking energetic.

I sit up and scoot to the edge of the bed. "For heaven's sake, please shut that racket off," I yell over the blaring lyrics.

"I'll turn it down," she shouts.

She returns and hands me a mug. I sip the hot liquid, moaning as the deliciousness erupts over my taste buds.

"Chop-chop, slowpoke."

"Jeez, can I drink my coffee first?"

"Yeah, just hurry the hell up."

"I'll chug it down and scorch my esophagus," I deadpan, sarcasm clear in my tone.

"Great." She beams, skipping out the door.

"Breakfast?" I call after her.

"We'll grab something before we hit the stores."

"Cool beans."

Mia glances at the grocery list, then dumps three big bags of potato chips in the shopping cart already loaded with a couple hundred dollars' worth of food.

"Are we feeding an army?" I gesture towards said items. "How many people did you invite to this shindig?"

"Around thirty, give or take a few."

"Really, Mia?"

"What?" she asks innocently.

"The apartment isn't big enough to accommodate that many people."

"You worry too much. It'll be fine."

"Mm-hmm."

"You should invite Daddy Dom. It'd be great to finally meet his psycho ass."

"I did," I hedge.

"And?"

"He doesn't want to come."

"Why?" Mia asks, indignant. "I throw the best parties."

"It's just not his thing. Anyway, his perpetual scowl would scare everyone."

"Good point. I can't have him mean-mugging our guests."

Dom hasn't been over, and I've only stayed the night at his place twice this week. He became somewhat distant after we came back from the island. Though Friday is the last day for interns, technically summer doesn't end until September. So we still have a month and a half together. By then he'll realize we're good for each other. Our relationship is violent… unconventional, but I love him. I wouldn't dare say those words to him, though. The old adage is true—love does hurt, but it's a hurt so sweet. All I can do is hope for the best.

"Patrick wants to come."

"Definitely no."

"Please, Mia."

"It's an adult party."

"Have a heart." I pout.

"All right." She sighs. "But I'm giving him the boot if he causes any trouble."

"Deal."

"Where are the Ritz crackers?" Mia scans the shelves. "Shouldn't they be in this aisle?"

"It's the next one."

We make our way over to the carb-laced snack.

"I can't believe classes start in a week. I'm so not prepared."

"I am."

"You would be, nerd."

"A title I gladly accept. Thanks for the compliment."

"I'm having fun before responsibility kicks me in the heinie." Mia plucks a box of crackers off the shelf and tosses it into the cart. "So tonight, I'm getting super drunk and riding some dicks."

"I'm not cleaning up your vomit."

"Yes, you are, because you wuv me." She kisses my cheek.

"Yeah, yeah." It's good having Mia back, even though she's a handful. "What else is on the list?"

"That was the last thing."

We head to the cash register.

"Where to next?"

"Liquor store."

"Yippee."

"Turn your frown upside down. We're finishing what we started in Denver."

"Yeah, but it ended in my kidnapping."

"Boo-hoo, cry me a river. I wish a gazillionaire took me to a private island and fucked my vagina raw."

After our initial clash, we spent the remaining days walking the beach, swimming in the ocean, and having hot sweaty animal sex. We even went to the mainland and bought a few souvenirs.

"Dude is totally *Stalking Laura* obsessed," Mia says matter-of-factly. "He's not going to let you go."

"You think so?" I ask, hope blooming in my chest.

"Oh God, your face lit up like a Christmas tree. You're a goner."

I was a goner the first time I laid my eyes on Dominic Stone.

Pepper

The mouthwatering aroma of frying bacon, potatoes, and French toast fills the kitchen. I got up a little while ago to cook breakfast. It's almost eleven o'clock, and I haven't heard a peep out of Mia. She'll be in bed recovering from a massive hangover all day. I'll peek in on her later. The party was still in full swing when I hit the hay. Patrick left before I went to my room. I guess the crowd wasn't his cup of tea. I put earplugs in and dozed off in no time. I woke to a messy apartment. It'll take hours to clean, but at least drunken bodies didn't litter the floor. That's a plus in my book. A bit later, I'm going to head to Dom's.

"Morning, sexy."

Screaming, I spin around, holding a hand to my chest.

A guy clad only in a pair of jeans openly ogles me. The denim hangs low on his lean hips, showcasing downy hair and a hard V leading to his private area.

"My apologies for scaring you." He motions behind me. "I hope there's enough to share."

"There isn't, sorry."

His gaze strays between my thighs.

"Nice panties," he says, a come-hither grin on his face

"Hey, eyes up here, buddy."

"I'm Peter, by the way," he introduces himself, licking his lips. "And you are?"

"Is Mia up?"

"Who's Mia?" He looks perplexed.

"The girl you banged last night."

"Oh yeah, I'm not good with names," he says sheepishly. "She's still sleeping."

Mia and I need to have a serious talk. She promised her one-night stands would be gone by sunrise.

"Peter, you have to leave."

"Are you sure?" he asks seductively.

"Yes," I snap, storming past him and barging into Mia's bedroom. "Oh my God."

A man is sprawled next to Mia on the bed, and another lies on the floor beside it. All are buck naked and appear comatose.

"Your friend is a tiger in the sheets." Peter slides his finger along the shell of my ear. "Are you wild as her?"

I elbow him in the stomach. "Get your stuff and go."

"Your loss." He shrugs, squeezing by me.

I whistle. "Rise and shine!"

Mia pops up and leans over the side of the bed, puking on the poor guy lying there. It's the chunky kind. Good grief, here we go again.

This morning was a circus. After disbanding the guys, I helped Mia shower, then cleaned up the stinky vomit as best I could. We'll need to buy a carpet shampooer to get rid of the stain. In the chaos, I forgot about cooking breakfast and the fire alarm went off, but by then it was too late; the bacon was burned to a crisp. I gave Mia a slice of wheat toast, orange juice, and a couple of ibuprofens before putting her back to bed.

As I'm gathering discarded Solo cups and other miscellaneous trash around the apartment, a loud bang sounds at the door.

"Pepper, it's me!" Patrick shouts. "Let me in!"

I swing the door open. "Where's the fire?"

"At the church." He pushes by me.

"What?" I ask, alarmed.

"I called you back-to-back." He paces the floor.

"I didn't hear my phone ringing." I walk over to him and take ahold of his arm. "Patrick, what's going on?"

"Earl knows everything."

"How did he find out?"

"No clue. He confronted Dad at church, in front of everyone."

"We knew this day was coming."

"But not this soon. It's surreal," he says, distressed.

"Calm down." I pull him to the sofa. "Sit."

I tuck my legs beneath me and face him.

"People were yelling and fighting. It was a mess."

"What did Dad do?"

"He played the victim and preached the merits of forgiveness. Oh, then he gave a half-assed apology. Most of the members didn't buy his bullshit and left."

"Did you see Lisa?"

"Yeah."

"How is she?"

"So much was happening, I didn't get a chance to speak to her."

"What a nightmare." I sigh. "I'll check on her later." I'm sure she's too busy dealing with family drama right now to talk.

"I hate him."

"Patrick—"

"No, Pepper. Don't try to redeem him. He's a horrible person."

"I know he is, but he's our father."

"I can't stand the sight of him."

"You'll be gone in two weeks."

"Can I crash here until then?"

"He won't like that."

"I'd rather sleep on the streets than to go back there," he says, determination etched on his face.

"I'll talk to Mia."

"Appreciate it."

"Anything for you. Want some lunch?" Food in his belly always lifts his spirits.

"Yeah."

"Any requests?"

"Cheesesteak and French fries."

"You got it." I squeeze his hand in solidarity. "We'll be okay."

He nods.

With my father's secret being exposed, the blackmailing scheme is over. The whole thing left a bitter taste in my mouth anyway. I'll work my butt off and apply for loans to pay for school.

CHAPTER 34

Pepper

Today a luncheon was given in honor of it being the last day for interns. Dom said a few words, mingled for a while, then left. I barely saw him this week. My intuition is blaring that something is wrong. I watched him the entire time, willing him to look at me, but he didn't—not once. I stopped by his office to put my concerns to rest, but he wasn't there. My worst fear was confirmed after I arrived home to find my diary laid primly on my pillow and atop it, a gold cross pendant necklace resembling the one Dom broke. Phone calls and texts to him went unanswered. Throwing my dignity to the wind, I searched for Drew's profile on Facebook and messaged him my cell number, asking him to call me. I sit cross-legged on my bed and impatiently wait. Within twenty minutes, my phone rings.

"Hey," I answer.

"Hi, Pepper, is everything okay?"

"Have you seen or spoken to Dom today?"

"I haven't spoken to him for a few weeks now."

"Why?"

"We had a bit of a falling-out."

"Because of me?"

"No, because he's a giant asswipe."

"Can you do me a favor?"

"Yeah."

"Tell Dom to call me right now. It's urgent."

"Pepper—"

"Please, he's ignoring me."

"That fucking prick."

"I love him."

"It won't make a difference."

"I'm begging you."

"Okay," he reluctantly agrees. "I'll call you back."

In less than five minutes, my cell rings again.

"Hello."

"I'm so sorry," Drew says, melancholy in his voice.

"What did he say?"

"Forget him, Pepper, and move on with your life."

"I need to know… for closure."

"He doesn't want to see or talk to you again," he says dismally. "If you need me, I'm just a call away.

"Thanks." I end the call.

I curl into a ball and cry for my broken heart. Why does this hurt so badly?

"Sweet pea, what's wrong?" Mia sits on the bed and pulls my head onto her lap.

In my despair, I didn't hear her come home.

"Dom doesn't want me anymore!" I wail, burying my face into her stomach.

"Screw him. You're too good for that bastard anyway."

I grab my keys from the nightstand and make a beeline for the front door.

"Where are you going?" Mia asks, right on my heels.

"To confront him. He doesn't get to end it this way."

She snatches the keys from my grasp.

I whirl on her. "What are you doing?"

"I can't let you go."

"Give me the fucking keys!" I scream.

"No," she says, holding them behind her back.

"Fuck you, Mia! You're not my goddamn mother!"

"It's for your own good."

"I love him." Tears roll down my cheeks. "You wouldn't understand because you're a whore who fucks anybody."

"If you go to him, by morning, you'll hate yourself."

"I don't care."

"Well, I do."

"I'm dying inside!" I sink to the floor. "I can't be without him."

Mia gets on her knees and wraps me in her embrace. "Losing your first love is the most painful, but trust me, it'll get better."

"How would you know? You've never been in love."

"Devin Scott," Mia blurts. "It's strange saying his name out loud."

"Who is he?"

"The only guy I ever gave my heart to. I was a nobody in high school before moving to Denver junior year and reinventing myself. The popular kids bullied me every damn day."

"Why didn't you tell me?"

"Shame. I killed my pathetic former self and wanted that spineless bitch to stay buried."

"What happened?"

"Devin asked me to the fall dance, and I thought I was the luckiest girl in the world." She snorts. "He was a senior, captain of the football team, and the worst of them all. No matter how badly he treated me, I held a torch for him like a fucking idiot."

Mia starts crying, and it's my turn to console her.

"After the dance, he took me to a wooded area and professed his undying love for me. I believed him." She laughs scornfully. "That night, I lost my virginity on the cold hard ground. His friends recorded it, and by the following day, I became the local celebrity."

"Were charges filed?"

"No. Football rules the small town where I'm from, and his father's an important man. The incident was swept under the rug, and my parents decided to relocate for a fresh start."

"Sorry for calling you a whore."

"It's already forgotten."

"You're an amazing friend."

"I'll always be here for you."

"Thank you."

"Let's get off the floor and dry our faces before Patrick shows up."

"Good idea."

"I'll gladly take a fork, sneak into Stone Incorporated, and stab the asshole's other hand. Just say the word."

"Mia…"

"Too soon?"

CHAPTER 35

Dom

Pepper called and texted all weekend, but I held firm on my decision. She made me fucking weak, becoming an addiction I grew dependent on and was slowly losing my sanity to. Blind jealously almost caused me to commit a double homicide in Denver. Rage, obsession, and passion combined, creating a lethal maelstrom inside me. We both nearly drowned because of it. At the island, the line separating Pepper and me blurred, complicating things. I knew our time together was over.

Today I got to work at the break of dawn, hoping to clear my mind of her by immersing myself in tedious tasks, but I can't concentrate. I'll fuck my way through countless women to expunge Pepper from my system. Soon, she'll be a distant memory. A knock at the door interrupts my thoughts. I asked not to be disturbed. Is that too much to fucking ask for?

"Come in," I bark, ready to tear someone a new asshole.

Peggy, my assistant, enters. She's accustomed to my abrupt moods and doesn't bat an eyelash at my obvious displeasure.

"Sandy Rucker is here to see you regarding an important matter."

"Were my instructions not clear to you?" I ask between clenched teeth.

"Ms. Rucker refuses to leave without personally delivering," Peggy clears her throat, "a package she says belongs to you."

I rub my temples, quickly losing my patience. "Send her in."

The woman trudges into my office, lugging a fussy baby in a car seat. The overwhelming stench of cheap perfume and alcohol assail my nostrils. Bloodshot eyes regard me from a haggard face caked in heavy makeup. Her black hair resembles a bird's nest, and she's dressed like she spent the night on a street corner bartering her carnal services.

"Can I help you?"

"This is Hunter, your son," she says in a voice raspy from years of smoking cigarettes.

"Excuse me?"

"My daughter, the fucking tart, disappeared yesterday." She drops the car seat on my desk. "I didn't raise my own damn brat, so I sure as hell ain't taking care of this one. That's your job, Daddy."

"You have the wrong man."

"Does the name Lauren Halstead ring a bell?"

"She told me her mother died."

"That's no surprise. The selfish bitch and me never got along."

I study the wiggling infant. He has my tawny blond hair and amber eye color. Doesn't mean I'm his father, but there's a small chance I could be. Recanalization can happen years after a vasectomy, though it's rare.

"Lauren's ploy was to use Hunter as her meal ticket, but she found some old rich fart to swindle and jumped ship."

"Any idea where she is?"

"Nope. I have to get going, so adios."

"Who's the man she ran off with?"

"Not a clue. Have a nice life." She rushes from the room.

Peggy steps in the doorway, an apprehensive expression mars her features. "Pepper Bryant is here."

"Goddamn it!" I shout, startling Hunter, who begins to cry. "Shit. Stay here and watch the baby."

I stalk from my office and round the corner. Pepper waits by Peggy's station. Eyes, puffy from crying, stare at me. Unruly curls frame her angelic face. An oversized T-shirt covered in stains and sweatpants hide her lush curves. Dirty white house slippers don her feet. It's plain to see she hasn't showered, but fuck, she's still the most beautiful woman I've ever seen.

"You shouldn't have come here."

"I need to talk to you."

I pull her into the nearest empty room. "You have two minutes."

"Do I mean anything to you?"

"No. Your novelty is gone."

"You're lying." Tears stream down her smooth face.

"You were a challenge," I say snidely. "A gullible church girl with daddy issues to corrupt."

"No!" Pepper wails. "You don't mean that!"

"It was very stupid of you to fill your head with fanciful notions."

"We belong together," she sobs. "Why won't you give us a chance?"

"For fuck's sake, Pepper!" I shout. "There is no us!"

"Don't do this. I'm different from Lauren and the other women you've dated."

I seize her throat in a bruising hold and jerk her to me, pressing my nose against hers. "It's. Fucking. Over."

"I'll do whatever you want," she cries hysterically. "I love you."

"You're fucking pathetic."

She throws her arms around my neck. "I can't lose you."

I roughly push her away, and she crumples to the floor. "Have some fucking dignity."

"Dom, please."

"Come here again and I'll have you tossed out on your ass." I leave her broken and crying.

"Aww, my grandbaby is so handsome," my mother coos. "Yes, you are."

Hunter giggles, flailing his chubby arms excitedly and blowing spit bubbles. My folks babysat while my lawyer and I met to discuss the next steps. Sandy Rucker abandoned Hunter without a bottle or a single diaper. I gave my mom and dad money to buy him the important baby essentials. I'll get the big stuff later. I parked my ass on the sofa and haven't moved since getting back. Pepper and the possibility of being a father plague my thoughts. She could be pregnant. The image of her midsection expanding with my child stirs my cock, and I refuse to examine the why.

"I may not be his father," I remind her.

"Bite your tongue. This is my grandchild." She protectively cradles him against her bosom. "He's the spitting image of you at this age."

"Your mother's right." Dad turns his attention from his favorite crime show to chime in. "There's no denying the strong Stone genes."

It's obvious they're already in love with him.

Jensen walks through the front door. "So, this is my nephew," he says, ruffling Hunter's tuft of hair.

"You two were supposed to keep quiet for now."

"He called and heard Hunter babbling," Mom says.

Drew comes in, and I give her a reproachful look.

"Since Jensen knows, there's no reason for Drew not to."

He's pissed at me, so I'm surprised he came.

"I'm going to start dinner," Mom says.

"I'll take him," Jensen offers.

Mom hands Hunter off and goes into the kitchen.

"Cute kid." Drew sits beside me.

"Thanks."

"I spoke to Pepper today," he says for my ears only.

"Not now."

"You fucking destroyed her, man. She's a wreck."

"She'll be fine."

"Do you love her? Jensen claims you do but said you're afraid of getting played again. I think you're just a fucking scumbag. Which is it?"

"I'm just a fucking scumbag."

"Maybe I'll ask her out and show her how a real man treats a woman."

"If we weren't in our parents' home, I'd knock you the fuck out."

"Did I hit a nerve?" he asks, smirking.

"Go near her and I'll rip your spleen from your body."

"Another man will tap that, eventually. Why can't it be me?"

"Shut your mouth," I seethe, ready to throttle the motherfucker.

"Her phat ass is fucking ripe." He licks his lips.

In an instant, I have Drew pinned to the wall by his shirt collar. "Touch her and you're dead."

"What the hell?" Jensen asks.

"Whoa, boys." Dad hops up and separates us. "Stop this before your mother sees."

"You're making a mistake, and when you realize that, it'll be too late," Drew says.

I let Drew go and storm outside to calm my tumultuous temper. Pepper is my tormentor. My desire for her far surpasses what I've ever felt for any woman. A passion this intense can only lead to a fatal conclusion. I had to end it to save her and myself, because if she were to betray me, I would kill her.

One month later

Pepper

"In ten minutes, I'm gone, Pepper," Patrick grumbles from the driver's seat. "I shouldn't even be here. I'm missing a friend's party tonight to see this asshole."

"Thank you for coming."

"Yeah, whatever."

"Hey, you just ran that stop sign."

"Sorry, didn't see it."

"Are you okay?" I ask.

"Yeah."

Patrick won't admit it, but he's nervous about seeing our father, and so am I. We haven't seen or spoken to him in several weeks. He called me the other day and asked to see us. It took some convincing, but Patrick agreed to drive down from school to support me.

"Russell should be in jail for the things he did to you."

"I shouldn't have told you."

"I'm glad you did. He needs to hang."

"Promise me you'll try to be receptive to whatever he has to say."

"You're asking for a lot."

"Pretty please." I bat my eyelashes.

"Fine." He pauses for a moment. "He deserves everything that's happening to him."

From Lisa we learned congregation numbers are dwindling fast, and Earl is suing Dad for ownership of the church. He and his wife are divorcing. Mary moved out, but Lisa chose to stay with Earl, who she recognizes as her father, despite DNA.

"We all eventually pay for our sins," I mumble.

"I was hoping to never step foot in this house again," Patrick says, parking in the driveway of our childhood home.

My stomach churns as I get out of the car. The front door opens and our father ambles onto the porch. Patrick shoves past him, not saying a word.

"Hi, Dad." I smile slightly.

"It's good to see you, Pepper."

I nod and go inside. Patrick leans against the wall, crossing his arms, and I sit on the sofa. A fearsome glower etches his face; so much for having an open mind. Dad stands in the middle of the living room. He's lost weight, and it's obvious he hasn't visited his barber in a while. I can't recall a time in my life he wasn't clean-shaven. Dirty dishes are stacked on the coffee table, and clothes, shoes, and other clutter are scattered across the floor. Church business and his legal troubles have taken a toll on him.

"Well, we're waiting, Russell," Patrick says, derision in his tone.

"I owe you both an apology."

"Keep your phony apology to yourself," Patrick scoffs.

"Let him talk."

I'm interested in what he has to say. Russell Bryant doesn't explain himself, ever, so this is a once-in-a-lifetime opportunity for me to understand what caused him to become an unfeeling tyrant.

"I've failed as a parent."

"Understatement of the century."

"Patrick, please—"

He cuts me off. "I can't listen to this bullshit."

"You have every right to be upset, but I vow to be a better father."

"So, because you had an epiphany all should be forgiven?" Patrick asks bitterly. "If your life wasn't in shambles, we wouldn't be having this conversation."

"I'm asking for a chance to make amends."

"Pepper told me about how you abused her."

Dad regards me solemnly. "You remind me of my mother."

Out of all the things he could've said, this was the least expected. Dad was raised by his grandmother.

She died long before Patrick and I were born. I've seen pictures of her and even heard a few stories, but any questions pertaining to his parents were strictly off-limits. They met their end when he was twelve, that's all I know.

"What's her name?" I ask.

"Anita Bryant."

"What was she like?" I bite my tongue, waiting on his answer.

"Charismatic, outgoing, and beautiful." He smiles sadly. "Everyone loved my mother and her baking too. She dreamed of owning a bakery one day. Her red velvet cake was my favorite."

"And Granddad?

"Everett was mean as a rattlesnake, abusive, and insecure. My father was a jealous man and convinced himself my mother was unfaithful. He beat her and me almost daily."

The other shoe has finally dropped. It all makes sense now. The abused became the abuser.

"You should've broken the cycle," Patrick says angrily.

"I prayed and prayed, seeking guidance, but I was weak."

"What happened to them?" I have an inkling their deaths were tragic.

"He came home drunk on a Saturday night, which wasn't uncommon, then the beating started. He punched her until she stopped moving, and I was powerless to help her." His eyes glaze over as he recounts the horrific details of my grandfather's violent crime. "Afterwards, he loaded his gun, pressed the barrel to his temple, and pulled the trigger. Blood and gore splattered my face. I kneeled beside my mother, held her hand, and waited for paramedics to arrive. She was pronounced dead on the scene. Blunt force trauma to the head was the official cause of death."

A lump forms in my throat and tears fill my eyes. Misfortune taints the Bryant lineage. Patrick slides down the wall, looking sick to his stomach.

"Why didn't you tell us?" My voice cracks.

"I wanted this buried and forgotten."

"This isn't something you keep from your children!" Patrick shouts.

"I thought it was for the best."

"You don't get to decide that!" Patrick jumps to his feet and storms out of the house.

"Can you forgive me for the way I treated you?"

"I will. Just give me time."

He nods. "I'll pay your college tuition and for anything else you need."

"Have you ever spoken to a therapist?"

"No."

"Can you? For me, please?"

"Yes, I promise."

"Thank you."

Consumed

This is a new beginning for my father, Patrick, and me.

CHAPTER 3.7

Pepper

Dom kneads my bottom while the tip of his tongue diligently explores my throbbing vulva. His proficient mouth fastens onto my swollen clit and sucks vigorously, creating an unbreakable suction that renders me incoherent. His long, tapered fingers tunnel through my pulsating portal, stimulating my G-spot. My sweaty body undulates, riding his face in rapture. The cool sheets stick to my heated skin. I'm a live wire, close to electrifying us both. My head thrashes from side to side, and my back arches as I orgasm.

Dom licks his way up my quivering belly and settles between my spread legs.

"I love you, Pepper." He kisses my lips and positions his thick manhood at my sopping entrance. "I'm sorry for hurting you."

"I love you too." Tears spill from my eyes. "Please never leave me again."

He gradually penetrates my center to the hilt. This man is my soul mate. He was born for me and I for him. Dom presses his forehead against mine and rolls his hips, plunging in and out of my depths. This play of his rippling, sleek muscles is spellbinding. I slide my hands over his hard flesh. If this is a sin, take me to Hell. I don't give a damn. I'll burn for him.

"Pepper, will you marry me?"

My eyes pop open, and I jolt up in bed.

A dream… it's just another dream.

I'm drenched in perspiration. My heart pounds in my chest, and my breathing is rapid. The sky beyond my window is pitch-black. I couldn't have been asleep long. As always, his touch felt so real. Dom haunts me. Asleep or awake, his presence surrounds me every single day. It's difficult to concentrate at work and school. My manager pulled me into his office to discuss customer complaints about incorrect orders, moving too slowly, and not being attentive. I was given a verbal warning, the first since starting the job freshman year. And the subpar assignments I've turned in have my professors side-eyeing me reprovingly. I delve my fingers beneath the waistband of my soaked panties and skim through my saturated folds. I moan, still feeling his length stroking inside me.

"Oh God!" I wail. "I can't take this torture anymore!"

I bury my face in my pillow and cry until I'm exhausted, but turbulent thoughts keep me awake. I roll over and grab my diary off the nightstand. The necklace Dom gifted me slips from between the pages and lands on my thigh. I pick it up and examine the intricate cross pendant. Our last encounter replays in my mind. I convinced myself if Dom saw me, he'd realize his mistake and confess his devotion and undying love. Instead, he thoroughly ruined me. The hurtful things he said cut me to the marrow. If Mia knew I went to see him, she'd wring my neck. Sometimes I stake out his office, hoping to catch sight of him, but it has proved fruitless.

Drew and I remain friends. We talk occasionally, but conversation regarding Dom is avoided. He's performing at a club this Friday night and invited Mia and me as VIP guests. I haven't seen him since the split with Dom. Sadness envelops me.

"How could you do this?"

I flounce out of bed and storm to the kitchen, determined to destroy any reminders of Dominic Stone. I flick the light on and throw the gold chain into the garbage disposal, then switch it on, mentally flipping him the bird. Hearing the metal being ripped apart is somewhat satisfying. Continuing my reign of destruction, I turn the burner on and tear pages from my diary. I hold them over the flame before flinging the burning paper into the sink. It's bittersweet watching my written desires become black ash. Dom brought those words to life. The waterworks start again. The pain of missing him is unbearable. It was stupid of me to think doing something so trivial would end it. Love is supposed to be beautiful, but for me it's agony. I wish I could sleep forever.

"Pepper, what's going on?" Mia rubs the sleep from her eyes and surveys the scene, concern evident in her expression. "I thought the apartment was on fire."

"I can't keep pretending I'm okay."

She hugs me. "It'll get better."

"Stop saying that," I sob, jerking away. "It hasn't."

"Give it time. It's only been a month," she says reassuringly.

"I'm reaching my breaking point." I slam my diary on the stove.

She pauses and regards me solemnly. "Remember the wager we made at the end of spring semester?"

Mia is a notorious slacker, and her GPA sucks because of it. She survived three years of college by luck and extra-credit work, aka giving up the goodies to the more unethical professors. I agreed to a blind date on the condition she aced her assignments and stayed on track when school started again. Surprisingly, she has.

"Yeah," I answer hesitantly, not liking the shift in topic.

"Welp, I'm collecting my debt," she says, turning off the garbage disposal and burner.

"That was before Dom."

"And?"

"I'm not ready to date."

"Too bad. I won the bet fair and square."

"It's wrong to string some poor guy along."

"I fucking hate seeing you like this," she says, hopping onto the counter.

"Dating won't help."

"I have the perfect guy for you. He's a jokester, super gorgeous, and charming. You two will click, guaranteed."

"No, Mia."

Why am I loyal to a man who discarded me?

You're fucking pathetic.

Dom's taunting words ring in my mind.

"Chill, babe, I'm not asking you to marry him. Dating doesn't have to be serious. It can be casual and fun. You could even gain a new friend."

"I'm not good company for anyone, and look where casual dating has gotten me."

"How do you expect to move on if you spend all your free time sulking at home?"

"No man will ever compare to him."

"Of course he hangs the moon and stars in your eyes. He's the only man you've been intimate with. You have no one to compare him to."

"I can't."

"Quit being so fucking stubborn. I can't stand hearing you cry yourself to sleep. Please, I'm begging you, just one date."

Guilt eats at me, and I hate it. Dom made it abundantly clear he doesn't want me. I should go and meet this guy. What could it hurt?

"I'm sure you haven't crossed Dom's mind once. He's living his life to the fullest and fucking other women."

"Okay," I relent. "One date."

"Deal!" she squeals. "I'll set it up for Saturday."

I have to do this, even though my heart rebels against it.

"This is cause for celebration." Mia takes a box of leftover pizza and a tub of vanilla ice cream from the fridge. She makes a cold pepperoni pizza and ice cream taco.

"You're really disgusting, Mia."

"Hey, don't knock it until you try it." She takes a big bite.

"I'll pass."

She shrugs. "More for me."

CHAPTER 38

Dom

I dive into my swimming pool and glide skillfully through the cold water. A DNA test confirmed Hunter is my son. Lauren was located in Dubai and readily relinquished her parental rights. A judge granted me temporary custody. I'm due in court soon to finalize custodianship. Hunter, though only six months old, is a handful and full of energy. The kid stays up practically all night giggling and babbling. Recently, he began teething, and it's driving me up the wall. At my mother's instructions, I've bought him an assortment of teether rings. He's fast becoming spoiled by my family and me. Truth be told, he's taken ahold of my heart. Since my mother is retired, she's been a great help, but I couldn't expect her to babysit Hunter every day, so I hired a nanny.

Finding the perfect person to care for him was strenuous. Countless interviews as well as background and reference checks took up the majority of my time for two straight weeks. I could have assigned someone to do the grunt work, but actively participating in decisions regarding Hunter is important to me. Finally, I settled on Emma Woodward. She has a bachelor's degree in early childhood development and a master's in education. At fifty-six years old, she's lively and vigorous. She and Hunter bonded immediately. So far, she's been excellent. There were a dozen or so young, pretty women who applied for the position, but selecting one of them would have no doubt led to complications. Most openly flirted and wore revealing clothing suited for a night of barhopping. Having a tenacious woman trying to squirm her way into my bed is not welcomed. My concern is for Hunter's well-being. He will receive the absolute best of everything.

I reach the end of the pool and do a tumble turn. Though I've been preoccupied, my thoughts constantly drift to Pepper. Incapable of expelling her from my mind, I followed her more than once, watching her while she worked, studied at the library, and completed other various tasks. Recalling her soft flesh, melodic voice, and the tight clasp of her wet pussy hardens my cock. Holding her panties to my nose as I jerk off is my favorite pastime. Lately, it hasn't quenched my sexual appetite. I'm in need of pussy. I haven't fucked another woman since her, but that'll be rectified tonight.

Drew refused to speak to me after the Pepper situation, but ultimately, we reconciled. Our relationship is still strained. He's adamant I should've given her a chance, but we don't dwell on the subject. My sudden fatherhood solidifies I made the right decision. Hunter is my top priority. Pepper is twenty-one and has her whole life ahead of her. She isn't ready for the responsibility of dating a man saddled with a baby. I catch a glimpse of Emma's snow-white hair in my periphery. She stands at the edge of the pool, holding a wiggling Hunter.

"Hunter just woke from his nap and could use some exercise before his snack."

I swim over to them, and she hands him to me. "Hey, buddy, ready for a dip?"

Hunter squeals excitedly, flailing his arms and kicking his legs. It's a plus he loves the water; it makes bath time easy.

"I'll come back in fifteen minutes."

"Make it twenty."

"Will do," she replies and walks off.

My life changed in the blink of an eye, but I'm acclimating to parenthood.

Consumed

Lilith's hungry gaze regards me from across the elegantly set table. Almond-shaped eyes, alabaster-colored skin, long, flowing black hair, a tall graceful form, and her Chinese descent gives her an exotic quality. She resembles a porcelain doll. I'm sure there are many men vying for her affection. I gave her a ring, and she invited me to dinner at her place. I'm breaking my rule of never fucking the same woman twice, but I'm desperate. Pepper is an unhealthy obsession I will conquer. I arrived to a house lit by dozens of candles and a savory meal of Peking roasted duck, rice, and broccoli. It's quite delicious, but there's something else I'm yearning for.

"Is the food to your liking?" she asks.

"It's very tasty."

"Wait until you try dessert," Lilith purrs.

"Looking forward to it."

"I'm glad you called me." She bats her eyelashes. "What prompted you to?"

"Your exemplary mouth."

It's one of the reasons I contacted her versus the numerous other options. She aims to please, and her carnal depravity matches my own.

"You haven't seen anything yet." She smiles seductively, displaying straight white teeth. "I've learned new tricks."

"Have you?"

"Oh yeah. My fellatio skills are unparalleled."

"That's a hell of a boast."

"I'd be happy to show you." She licks her bottom lip.

I push the chair back. "Then what the fuck are you waiting for?"

She sashays to me, adding extra swagger in her steps. Her dark areolas and bald pussy are visible through her sheer red skintight dress. My dick doesn't rouse. What the fucking hell?

Lilith descends to her knees and slowly undoes my pants. "I miss sucking your big cock, Daddy."

Goddamn it, my dick doesn't stir.

"No worries, baby, I'll get you nice and stiff."

She twirls her velvet tongue around my bulbous head, but nothing. Shit, this has never happened to me before.

"You okay, baby?" Her face scrunches, forming a wrinkle between her eyebrows.

It's Pepper. I can't drive her from my fucking system.

"I have to go."

"Excuse me?" she screeches in indignation.

"It's not you." I stuff my flaccid dick into my pants and stand.

"Are you serious?"

"Thanks for dinner," I say, walking towards the door.

My cock is trained to only get hard for Pepper. Shit just got real.

CHAPTER 39

Pepper

Mia barges into my bedroom, places her hands on her hips, and taps her foot impatiently. "Shake a leg, Pepper."

As usual, she looks stunning. The cream-colored fishnet bralette displays her breasts, and the miniature orange leather shorts expose her butt cheeks. Seriously, those things could be mistaken for underwear. Four-inch Jimmy Choo pumps she spent months saving to buy grace her feet.

"Almost done." I face the mirror and continue massaging curling custard cream into my hair.

"Hurry," she demands. "Drew goes on in an hour."

Mia's nervous. She's trying to play it cool but is failing miserably. She's fangirl crushing hard on Drew.

"Ten minutes."

"You have five." She flips her bob and struts out of the room.

"Ms. Bossy Diva," I mumble.

"I heard that."

"You were meant to," I counter.

"Pepper Penelope Bryant, I'm dragging your ass out of this apartment in four minutes."

"All right," I say in exasperation.

My simple lime-green slip dress is less racy than Mia's getup. The transparent platform heels I wore on my birthday complete my outfit. Sudden flashbacks of Dom pounding between my legs while wearing the stripper-style shoes bombard me. My libido sparks to life, and my neglected center throbs, recalling every detail of my stay on the island. I grip the edge of the dresser and squeeze my thighs together. I'm in desperate need of a Dom fix. Tremors rack me as I'm overcome with the need for his kisses, his caresses… his barbaric domination. Initially, the violence of his claiming shocked me, but it has become my addiction. I crave the special brand of debauchery he inflicts on my body. Mia said I'm a masochist. In my ignorance, I didn't know what the term meant. Once she explained, it made perfect sense. Unquestionably, the desire for pain stems from my abusive childhood. Dom's a sadist, and I'm a masochist; we're two peas in a pod.

My determination from a week ago to sock it to Dom and demote him to my rearview fizzles. Maybe

I should cancel the date. I'm not ready, but Mia will surely kick me in the shins if I renege. She would only tell me the guy's name. What if we have nothing in common? The prospect of sitting through an awkward date makes me cringe. Mia even refused to show me a picture, stating, "It'll ruin the concept of a blind date." He could be a grotesque goblin. Okay, I admit Mia wouldn't set me up with a guy she considered unattractive or a douchebag, but any excuse will do to bail. Might as well tell her now. I blow out a breath and go into the living room.

"Finally." Mia grabs her clutch and hops up from the sofa.

"I'm having second thoughts—"

"I can't hear you." She slaps her hands over her ears. "La, la, la, la."

"Seriously, Mia."

"I'm not letting you weasel out of the date." She points a finger at me. "End of story."

"I'm kidding myself." I sigh sadly. "I'll never get over Dom."

"Doubts are expected, but it doesn't mean you get to change your mind. I love you, Pepper. You're more than a friend… you're my sister. I wouldn't push you to go if you didn't spend the last thirty days moping. Do you trust me?"

"Of course."

"Then stop overthinking and let's go. I'm ready to back this ass up on the dance floor all night."

The line to get into the upscale nightclub was several blocks long. Luckily, our VIP status allowed us to skip to the front and be taken inside to a roped-off section to watch Drew's performance. Boy, did he put on a show. He has an exceptional voice. The mob of people chanted his name, and when he appeared, a deafening roar filled the building. He hyped the crowd, prancing back and forth across the raised platform. Stardom suits him. I hung on to his every note and rocked my hips to the beat of the music. After singing five songs, Drew left the stage and was swallowed by the mass of bodies. Minutes later, a bouncer escorts Mia and me to the second floor. It's not jam-packed up here.

"Pepper." Drew grabs me in a bear hug and spins me around. "It's so good to see you."

"Yeah, you too, and you were amazing."

"Thanks." He puts me down and peers at Mia. "You must be the roommate."

"I am. My name is Mia."

"Well, it's nice to meet you, Mia." His gaze roams over her appreciatively. "Pretty pink shade of nipples you have."

She blushes a tomato red. "I'm glad you like them."

And cue the sexual tension thickening the air.

"Shall we sit?" Drew asks.

"Lead the way," Mia purrs.

I roll my eyes. Guess I'll be going home alone.

We follow him to a group of red plush leather chairs situated around a table. Drew introduces us to the people already seated. A server comes by and takes our orders. The three of us chat, but I'm mostly excluded from the conversation because Drew and Mia are too busy flirting. She's comfortably sitting in his lap now, feeding Drew olives as he openly gropes her. This is the quickest courtship I've seen.

"Pepper is over your dickhead brother. I'd be grateful if you could relay the message to him."

I shoot Mia a death glare.

"Is that so?"

"Absolutely. She has a date tomorrow night with a hunky stud."

"Shut up, Mia."

"I'm happy for you," Drew says genuinely.

"It's nothing serious," I say too quickly, as if I'm guilty of something. "Just testing the waters."

"I have to go the little girls' room." Mia stands.

Drew slaps her butt. "Hurry back."

"Will do, Daddy."

Give me a break.

I have a few minutes to gather information before Mia gets back. I shouldn't ask, but I'm desperate for an update.

I clear my throat. "How is he?"

"Forget him."

"Please, knowing will ease my mind."

"He has a lot on his plate."

"What happened?"

"He's a father now."

"What?" I croak.

Could it be Dom was in a relationship the whole time we were together?

"It's not what you're thinking."

Drew explains the situation, and honestly, I'm at a loss for words. How can a mother abandon her baby? Sadly, Dom has more motive to hate and be distrustful of women now more than ever.

CHAPTER 48

Pepper

I scan the restaurant in search of my date. It shouldn't be too hard to find a man sitting alone. I thought of Dom on the whole drive here. He plays a recurring role in my dreams nightly, and it's pushing me to the brink of madness. My mind is in turmoil, and my heart isn't in it, but Mia is right. I owe it to myself to move on.

"Pepper?" The deep Irish brogue prickles my skin.

I glance back and see an attractive redheaded man standing to the left of the entrance. He has the brightest green-blue eyes I've ever seen and a smattering of freckles across his nose.

"Yes, and you must be Finnegan."

"Please, call me Finn."

He leans in for a hug at the same time I offer my hand, and we shake awkwardly. Maybe I made a faux pas. I'm not accustomed to dating. Is hugging over a handshake the norm? I avert my eyes, too bashful to meet his gaze.

"Finn it is."

"The table is this way."

"Great, I'm starving."

I study his tall, broad frame as I follow behind him. This guy is solid muscle. In true gentleman fashion, Finn pulls out the chair for me, and I promptly sit.

"Thank you." His masculine, woodsy scent is mouthwatering.

"You're welcome."

I pick up the menu. "Have you eaten here before?"

"I have. You?" he asks, settling in the chair opposite me.

"First time."

"You'll love it. Usually reservations for this place book weeks in advance, but I was lucky."

"What do you recommend?"

"The stuffed catfish is their signature dish and one of my favorites. It's drizzled in a garlic parmesan sauce."

"Yum, sounds delicious. I'll have that."

"You won't be disappointed."

After our orders are taken, we chitchat and discover we have common interests. We're both Cancers and love watching zombie movies. Like me, Finn detests cauliflower, so he's okay in my book. The food is brought to the table, and the conversation dies down. I eat a forkful of the succulent fish. My eyes flutter closed, and I moan as the flavor hits my taste buds. I open my eyes to find Finn watching me. His unwavering scrutiny makes me uncomfortable.

"Why are you staring at me?"

"You're a beautiful woman." He smiles, flaunting dimples.

My complexion hides my blush from his piercing perusal, and for that I am grateful.

"I wasn't keen on a blind date, but now I'm happy Mia convinced me to come," he says.

"How do you know her?"

"Through my sister, Maggie."

I remember meeting Maggie once, a while ago. She and Mia used to work together at a department store during freshman and sophomore year. We eat and talk more. By the end of the meal, all my misgivings are gone. I'm having an awesome time, and there's budding chemistry between us. Finn is a jokester, as Mia said, though some of his jokes are corny. It's wonderful to genuinely laugh. Dom is still at the forefront of my mind, but not blaringly so. I become bold, elated at the prospect of expelling him completely from my thoughts. I'm done being miserable and feeling empty inside every day.

"Would you like to watch a zombie movie at my place?"

"Sure." Finn readily accepts the invitation.

Dom

I watch the vibrant colors light up the sky as the sun sets while lounging in the wicker chair on Jensen's wooden deck. Hunter rests comfortably in my lap. Sarah and the kids went to see a movie and will be arriving home any minute now. The girls asked to see Hunter today. I'm here or at my parents' house more times than not. Hunter is the center of attention in the family. He will never lack love.

Jensen opens the screen door that leads to the kitchen and steps onto the patio, holding two beers. He gives me one, then sits beside me. Hunter's little fingers and toes wiggle in excitement. He latches on to the cold bottle and tries to bring it to his mouth. For a six-month-old baby, he's strong.

"Whoa, buddy, this isn't for you. Underage drinking is against the law." I offer Hunter his pacifier instead, but he vehemently shakes his head and reaches for the bottle again. He just drank eight ounces of formula, so he can't be hungry.

"That's a baby for you." Jensen chuckles. "Always wanting what they can't have."

I tickle Hunter's soft belly and kiss his cheek. He giggles and releases a wet fart. I hope this isn't another blowout. Yesterday, shit was everywhere.

"Whew!" Jensen covers his nose. "Rancid!"

I check his diaper. "He's good."

"You sure? He probably needs to see a specialist."

"Hunter's a stinker." I ruffle his hair.

"Fatherhood suits you," Jensen says, smiling ear to ear.

I dip my head in acknowledgment of his comment.

"I had a date last night."

"How'd it go?"

"I couldn't get an erection."

"Fuck, what's the problem?"

"Pepper. I let her go too soon."

"Well, you blew your chance."

"I'm paying her a visit tomorrow."

"You can't pop up and expect her to open her arms in welcome."

"That's exactly my expectations."

I'm back in the picture, and that's final. Pepper has no choice but to accept it.

Jensen rubs his nape. "Do you love her?"

I shrug and sip my beer.

"What are your intentions?"

"To keep her around until I'm tired of her."

"Pepper could be seeing someone."

"She isn't."

The GPS tracker is still installed in her cell phone. I monitor her movements often in addition to occasionally tailing her. Pepper hasn't deviated from her routine. It wouldn't have ended well if I saw her with another man.

"She's on a date right now."

"What the fuck did you say?" I see red, and instant rage eats away at me.

"Dom, you're too late."

"How do you know where she is?" I ask calmly, though I'm boiling inside. Shouting will scare Hunter.

"Leave it be."

"Jensen, you have ten seconds to talk before all hell breaks loose."

He releases a deep sigh and comes clean.

I kiss Hunter on the forehead and hand him to Jensen. "See you later, champ."

Jensen grasps my forearm. "Don't do anything stupid."

"I'm claiming what's mine, and fuck the consequences."

Pepper

"Moron! Why did you go outside?" I yell at the television, throwing my hands up in frustration. "Now you'll die horribly, and you deserve it too."

Finn laughs at my outburst. We sit on the couch watching a group of Londoners fight for survival, a bowl of popcorn separates us. We're alone in the apartment. Drew and Mia are off somewhere getting busy most likely. Last night, they left the club together, and I haven't seen or heard from them since.

"Sorry." I smile sheepishly. "Evidently, I'm taking this movie way too seriously."

The guy left the safety of the house to investigate a strange *noise*. Everyone knows that's a big no-no in life-or-death situations, especially in a freaking zombie apocalypse. They're everywhere, and not the slow kind either. Sure enough, the man is devoured by four reanimated corpses. *Imbecile.*

"No apology necessary. I remember smashing the TV in a bar after my favorite rugby team lost."

"Well, I've never smashed a television." I chuckle.

We lapse into silence, eyes glued to the screen as the actors meet gruesome fates. He caresses my thigh, and I freeze. The touch is foreign. My instinct is to shy away from the intimate contact, but it's comforting, and I need to feel something besides desolation. The man I love rejected me. Finn can help me forget and is a perfect substitute. I aim to end the last thirty days of torture, tonight.

"Is this okay?"

"Yes," I reply breathlessly.

His hand moves upwards, sliding under my dress.

"If you want me to stop, just say the word."

I nod, leaning against the cushions. Finn skims his fingers along the edge of my panties. In the back of my mind, alarm bells boom. I ignore them, refusing to be swayed. If I have to seek pleasure elsewhere to move on, so be it. Finn gets on his knees and tugs my underwear off. I open myself to him, hoping he can transport me to the same erotic heights as my former lover. His tongue probes my labia. The siren in my head grows louder. My quest to reach orgasm is hampered by thoughts of Dom swamping me. This isn't working. I should've known Dom would be irreplaceable. Before I can put a halt to my idiotic plan, there's a loud bang and the front door flies open. Dom looms in the entryway, snarling like a rabid dog. His glowering countenance strikes terror in me. Danger thickens the surrounding air. It's so palpable, the rancid taste of it clogs my esophagus.

"Who the fuck is this asshole?" Finn asks, anger lining his words.

Dom's feral gaze zooms in on him, and he races towards us at top speed, unleashing a spine-chilling bellow. He catapults over the sofa, tackling Finn. They crash into the coffee table, obliterating the small wooden piece of furniture. The bowl of popcorn falls onto the carpet. Dom delivers a blow to Finn's nose, and I hear a sickening crunch. The alpha males clash in a tangle of limbs, pummeling one another, but it's apparent who'll be the victor. Finn's brawn is no match for Dom's wrath. He's quickly demoted to beta.

"Dom, stop it!"

Finn is getting beaten to black and blue. Dom leaps up and kicks him in the abdomen repeatedly. Blood spews from his nose and mouth. I'm to blame for putting him in this situation. I have to do something.

"You're killing him!" I shout, launching myself onto Don's back.

I'm effortlessly dislodged and hurled into the television. The forty-inch set careens to the floor, and I land on top of it, causing the screen to shatter on impact. Excruciating pain explodes in my shoulder. I think it's dislocated.

"Your ass whooping is next," he growls.

Finn uses the distraction to gather his senses and rise to his feet. He decks Dom across the temple. An elbow to the ribs followed by a jab to the gut is dealt swiftly in reprisal. Finn bends over, clutching his midsection. Dom takes advantage of his position and knees him in the face. Finn topples to the floor. I crawl to a safe spot and cradle my sore arm to my chest. I close my eyes and pray Finn lives to see tomorrow. The thrashing continues. I gag, listening to the vicious assault. Seconds, minutes, or hours could've passed. Eventually, blessed silence greets my ears. Is Finn dead, departing this world via a violent crime of passion? His spirit will surely haunt me for the rest of my days. Dare I confirm my fears? I count to ten and risk a peek. Dom towers above Finn's prone form, but he's breathing.

Thank God.

"You're alive because your pants are on, but come near my property again, I'll fry your balls and feed them to you." Dom drags him to the door and tosses him out, then slams it shut again.

Dom

My prey cowers in the corner, knees drawn to her chest, frightened as a rabbit snared by a ravenous fox.

Her trepidation is warranted. She lied and attempted to give away what belongs to me. I wouldn't have found Pepper in this predicament had her proclamation of love held merit. The penalty for her transgressions is steep. Collection is due, and the only acceptable restitution is her withering in agony. Then I'll be appeased.

"Your love expired in four weeks," I grit out, visibly vibrating in fury.

"No." Crocodile tears gleam in her eyes. "I still love you."

"Lying whore!" I roar, flipping the sofa.

"I needed to forget." Her voice wobbles. "Constantly thinking of you drove me crazy."

Pepper has the ability to wrap me around her finger. How could I allow myself to fall under the spell of another conniving bitch? Unable to get a handle on my jumbled emotions, I punch holes into the wall.

"I missed you so much," she sobs. "Please believe me."

I storm into the kitchen and grab a knife, then go back to the living room. Pepper zeros in on my hand. To escape the apartment, she has to bypass me. She chooses the safer route and scurries to her bedroom, but a locked door won't impede my revenge. A well-placed kick grants me access. She fumbles with her cell phone, struggling to dial 9-1-1 in her frantic state. I snatch the wireless device from her grasp and pitch it across the room. It smacks into the mirror, sending shards of glass and pieces of the mobile in every direction. She makes a run for it, but her bid for freedom is short-lived. I seize her hair and fling her onto the bed.

"My shoulder!" she wails.

I jump on behind her and slice the blade through her dress, cutting her in the process. I cast the tattered garment onto the carpet.

"You're upset." Pepper shakes like a leaf. "Don't do something you'll regret."

"You were going to fuck him." I place the tip of the blade at her clit.

She caresses my cheek. "I couldn't, because I love you."

"Your love is weak," I bark, driving the sharp point forward.

Blood gushes from the small nick.

"Please, stop!" she cries hysterically.

I drag the knife up her quivering torso and nudge the honed edge against her throat, drawing blood. "A flick of my wrist would sever your carotid artery, and you'd bleed to death in minutes."

"What are you waiting for, huh?" she screams. "Do it, you fucking bastard! I'm sick of your bullshit!"

I press my nose to hers, and instantly her sweet vanilla scent envelops me. It acts as an aphrodisiac, stiffening my cock. A war wages inside my heart. It's been too fucking long since I've smelled her... tasted her... felt the grip of her pussy on my dick. My need to hurt her equals my desire to fuck her.

"You spurned my love, and you have the audacity to be angry?" she yells.

"I'm back and the same rules apply."

"Fuck your rules and fuck you too."

"You've forgotten who's in charge." I dig the knife deeper into her soft skin. "I'm happy to fuck you into submission."

She whimpers but refuses to heel. "I'm my own woman, and I demand you leave my apartment."

"You're mine." I undo the clasp of my jeans and free my aching length. "Whether you agree or not."

"The hell I am. You crushed my soul."

"We can do this the easy way or the hard way, but I'm never letting you go." I glide the head of my manhood through her bloody slit. "You have my word."

"I'm supposed to trust you?" she whispers, moaning.

I slash my palm and stroke my bulging arousal, covering it in my life's source. "A blood oath binds my declaration."

My tongue dips into the recesses of Pepper's tantalizing mouth, capturing her silken lips in a voracious kiss. She feverishly matches my hunger. I guide her legs to my shoulders and brutally push inside her heated wetness, my weapon discarded.

Groaning, I bury my face into the curve of her neck. All semblance of my humanity vanishes, and I regress to a primitive state, reversing eons of evolution in a matter of seconds. The urgency to fuck her into oblivion thrums in my veins.

"Is this a dream?" Her warm breath grazes my ear. "If it is, never wake me."

My thoughts echo Pepper's sentiments. This can't be real; maybe it isn't. Perhaps we're in a parallel universe where reality is warped. How else did this slip of a girl tie me in knots? Train my cock to only harden for her delectable cunt?

"If you ever betray me, I'll kill you and damn us both," I slur, drowning in her pussy.

My hips piston between her thighs, mindless in my pursuit to bathe her cervix in my semen, unequivocally marking my possession. Grunts, heavy breathing, and the salacious harmony of sweaty flesh resonate in the room. My ruthless thrusts drive our intertwined bodies over the side of the bed. I latch on to her ankles and spread her wide, surging forward relentlessly. Pepper's petite channel convulses, and I pump faster, spurting cum into her sopping core. We shout, climaxing together.

"More," I rasp, rolling Pepper to her stomach.

"Yes, more," she pants.

I lie on top of her and work my straining erection into her snug rectum. Tonight, neither of us will sleep. By morning, she'll be fucked raw and I'll be wrung dry. I grind against her plump ass, bludgeoning her tight hole. She writhes and twists beneath my onslaught. I wedge my hand between her blood-soaked folds and tease the center of her pleasure.

"Dom!" she screams, orgasming.

"I love you," I murmur, spilling my seed inside her.

I finally say aloud what I've known for a while but kept denying. What I felt for Lauren is trivial compared to the scope of emotions Pepper brings to life inside me. My passion for her could lead to disastrous consequences, but fuck it. I need her by my side, always. I fought loving her and made accusations I knew weren't justified. My net worth and my burned face don't matter to her.

"I love you, too."

Nine years later

Pepper

Stone Incorporated has successfully acquired BSY, a big technology organization. Our lawyer is preparing a contract to be signed tomorrow. Other companies were interested in purchasing the business, so we had to act fast or risk losing the opportunity to further diversify Stone Inc. My assistant, Janet, and I arrived in Melbourne, Australia, late last night on a private airplane. This morning we met with the board of directors to discuss the mutual benefits of the acquisition. Jetlagged from the flight, Janet opted to go to her hotel room, while I chose to have a celebratory glass of wine at the five-star restaurant located in the lobby. This deal will quadruple the holdings of Stone Incorporated, which I am now co-owner of.

Dom's name flashes across the screen of my cell phone, and I press Decline, probably for the hundredth time. We tied the knot eight and a half years ago, a couple months before the birth of our first child. I walked across the stage to collect my college degree with a bulging belly. We're the proud parents of four, including Hunter, whom I adopted. For all intents and purposes, I am his mother. He's nine, Brielle eight, Carmen five, and Knox just turned one. Dom's a great father, but being the wife of a domineering man is challenging, to say the least. There's never a dull moment. But I'm no longer a timid virgin. I'm confident and refuse to bite my tongue during arguments. This infuriates him, and we end up fucking like wild animals. Eventually, he overcame his aversion to looking at himself in the mirror which greatly pleased me.

Dom was due to attend this meeting in two days, but I changed the date and time. He's livid, but echoing his favorite statement to me, *you'll get over it*. I'm a mother and a career woman, something he fails to understand. He gives me the remedial tasks to handle, as if I'm some incompetent intern. My skills landed us a billion-dollar increase in revenue. I needed to show him I'm his partner in every sense of the word, at home and in the office.

Besides that, I love my life. I go to church regularly with the children, and sometimes Dom joins us. Patrick is a successful sports agent. Lisa signed to a modeling agency and relocated to Paris. We're still very close. I visit my father on occasion and bring the kids along. He has severe health problems and is under the care of a twenty-four-hour nurse. It took a while, but Patrick has finally forgiven him. My mobile rings, displaying Mia's name.

"Hello."

"The wedding is off!" she shouts, voice thick with tears. "I found some skank's panties in Drew's bedroom!"

Drew and Mia are engaged after a tumultuous on-and-off-again courtship. They're in the process of planning a Halloween-themed wedding and closing on a mansion. Currently, they live separately.

"I'm sure there's a reasonable explanation." Drew may be a lot of things, but a cheater isn't one of them. "Have you spoken to him?"

She comes to me for relationship advice often, which is a drastic change. This is the sort of guidance I used to seek from her.

"No, I left before he got in." She sniffles. "I can't talk to him."

"Where are you?"

"Heading home."

"Calm down, then call him. Drew wouldn't be unfaithful to you."

"You really think so?"

"Of course. He is a good man," I assure her.

"Okay."

"Give me a buzz later." I end the call.

I sigh as my ringtone blares again.

"Hi, Drew."

"Hey. Have you heard from Mia? I keep getting her voicemail."

"Yep. She's pissed because she found some woman's panties in your bedroom."

"Fuck, she has the wrong idea. I let a buddy crash at my place on Saturday night since I had a gig in Vegas and his house was being fumigated."

"Swing by her place and explain."

"I appreciate the heads-up."

"No problem."

I gulp down the rest of my wine.

The waiter appears. "Would you like another glass?"

"Three is enough. Thank you."

I pay the bill and stumble to the elevator, a bit tipsy. Surprisingly, I make it to my room without falling flat on my face.

After a few clumsy attempts, I insert the key card into the electronic slot.

"Success." I giggle and push the door open.

I'm ambushed the moment I step inside and dragged through the dark suite. *Dom.* I didn't expect him so soon. I'm thrown on the bed. My hands and ankles are quickly restrained with zip ties and then I'm flipped to my back.

"Pepper, you've been a disobedient girl, and now there's hell to pay," Dom purrs.

"Give me your worst." I blow a kiss at him.

Moonlight shines into the room, revealing the glint of a knife and his white teeth as his lips form a sinister smile. "My pleasure."

THANK YOU FOR READING

It was so awesome writing Dom and Pepper's story. I hope you enjoyed it. Don't forget to leave a review and read my other books! Connect with me on social media:

Facebook – Author Lorrain Allen

Instagram – author_lorrain_allen

TikTok – authorlorrainallen

Twitter – AuthorLAllen

ABOUT THE AUTHOR

Lorrain Allen currently resides on the East Coast. She has one amazing, albeit spoiled, son. She loves to get away from the world by losing herself in a book. Her long-term goal is to pen dark, erotic, paranormal, contemporary, new adult, and young adult romances. The subject matters of her books are controversial, but what's life without a little controversy?

OTHER BOOKS

Standalones

Slippery When Wet: When Adults Play

The Games We Play

Consumed: A Dark Stalker Age Gap Romance

Maverick's Madness: A Dark High School Bully Romance

Living in Cin Duet

When Art Rises: Living in Cin (A Dark High School Romance)

When Art Falls: Living in Cin (A Dark Romance)

A Little Taste of Sin Series

Sweet Peach

Midas Touch

Gods of Ruin MC Series

Beautiful Hate: A Dark MC Romance

www.authorlorrainallen.com

Printed in Great Britain
by Amazon

80005217R00185